BERLIN FROM 25,000 FEET

Coming along into the flak over the city, a Fort in a wing off to our left pitched over into a screaming dive into the flame below. The plane was on fire. All four props were turning smoothly. Maybe the pilot had a personal grudge to settle, and wanted to make sure his bombs went home . . . or maybe the pilot was a bloody pulp in his seat, and the controls were shot away, and the co-pilot was a corpse, and the plane was afraid to stay up there any longer.

SERENADE TO THE BIG BIRD

"An earnest, wonderful and heartbreaking work—a young man's grim and loving tribute to his pals, his generation. It is not an easy book for me to say anything orderly about. It is deeply moving, that's all."

—*William Saroyan*

THE BANTAM WAR BOOK SERIES

This series of books is about a world on fire.

The carefully chosen volumes in the Bantam War Book Series cover the full dramatic sweep of World War II. Many are eyewitness accounts by the men who fought in a global conflict as the world's future hung in the balance. Fighter pilots, tank commanders and infantry captains, among many others, recount exploits of individual courage. They present vivid portraits of brave men, true stories of gallantry, moving sagas of survival and stark tragedies of untimely death.

In 1933 Nazi Germany marched to become an empire that was to last a thousand years. In only twelve years that empire was destroyed, and ever since, the country has been bisected by her conquerors. Italy relinquished her colonial lands, as did Japan. These were the losers. The winners also lost the empires they had so painfully seized over the centuries. And one, Russia, lost over twenty million dead.

Those wartime 1940s were a simple, even a hopeful time. Hats came in only two colors, white and black, and after an initial battering the Allied nations started on a long and laborious march toward victory. It was a time when sane men believed the world would evolve into a decent place, but, as with all futures, there was no one then who could really forecast the world that we know now.

There are many ways to think about that war. It has always been hard to understand the motivations and braveries of Axis soldiers fighting to enslave and dominate their neighbors. Yet it is impossible to know the hammer without the anvil, and to comprehend ourselves we must know the people we once fought against.

Through these books we can discover what it was like to take part in the war that was a final experience for nearly fifty million human beings. In so doing we may discover the strength to make a world as good as the one contained in those dreams and aspirations once believed by heroic men. We must understand our past as an honor to those dead who can no longer choose. They exchanged their lives in a hope for this future that we now inhabit. Though the fight took place many years ago, each of us remains as a living part of it.

SERENADE TO THE BIG BIRD

BERT STILES

BANTAM BOOKS
TORONTO · NEW YORK · LONDON · SYDNEY

SERENADE TO THE BIG BIRD

*A Bantam Book / published by arrangement with
W. W. Norton & Company, Inc.*

PRINTING HISTORY

*First published in the United States of America in 1952
by W. W. Norton*

Bantam edition / April 1984

Drawings by Greg Beecham, Tom Beecham and M. Stephen Bach.

Map by Alan McKnight.

ISBN 0-553-23985-6

Published simultaneously in the United States and Canada

PRINTED IN THE UNITED STATES OF AMERICA

O   0 9 8 7 6 5 4 3 2 1

This book is dedicated to
MAC
who was a good guy
who went down when I was on pass
in London . . . having a good time

CONTENTS

SERENADE
TO THE
BIG BIRD

WESTERN EUROPE

Scale of Miles

0   100   200   300   400

Stornov

Isle of Sky

Inverne

SCOTLAN

IRELAND

GREA
BRITA

Coventry

Cambridge

Londo

ATLANTIC   OCEAN

Land's End

hering Cross

English Channel

Cherbourg

Abbev

Le

Lorient

NORMANDY

Seine

BAY OF
BISCAY

Loire R.   Orleans

Tour

Avor

FRAN

SPAIN

Lisbon

MEDITERRAN

FIRST CREW

1st Lieut. Samuel Newton, Pilot. 23 years old, of
Sioux City, Iowa.

1st Lieut. Bert Stiles, Co-pilot. 23 years old, of
Denver, Colorado.

1st Lieut. Donald M. Bird, Bombardier. 24 years
old, of Oswego, New York.

1st Lieut. Grant H. Benson, Navigator. 22 years
old, of Stambaugh, Michigan.

T/Sgt. William F. Lewis, Engineer. 20 years old,
of Grand Island, Nebraska.

T/Sgt. Edwin C. Ross, Radio Operator. 23 years
old, of Buffalo, New York.

S/Sgt. Gilbert D. Spaugh, Toggleer. 21 years old,
of Winston-Salem, North Carolina.

S/Sgt. Gordon E. Beach, Ball-turret gunner. 34
years old, of Denver, Colorado.

S/Sgt. Basil J. Crone, Waist-gunner. 24 years old,
of Wichita, Kansas.

SERENADE TO THE BIG BIRD

S/Sgt. Edward L. Sharpe, Tail-gunner. 21 years
old, of Hot Springs, Arkansas.

Sam and I both went to Colorado College in Colorado
Springs, and were fraternity brothers. Neither of us did
very much except play around at school before we went to
the cadets. It was pure luck that we ran into each other in
Salt Lake City. We finally talked some WAC into putting
us on the same crew.

Don used to work in a bank before the war. He
joined the crew in the middle of phase training at
Alexandria, Louisiana. He was a bombardier-instructor
and he didn't have to go to war at all, but he wanted to see
what a war is like and he wanted to wear the ETO ribbon
with a star on it.

Grant went to school for a while at Michigan State
before the war, and knocked around the country, and did
a stretch in the infantry before he became a navigator. He
joined the crew in Alexandria also.

Lewis drove a cab in Grand Island before the war,
and ran around with a girl there, and spent a lot of time
wishing he was back.

Ross was some sort of clerk in the daytime in civilian
days, and a big-time operator at night. When the crews
were cut from ten to nine men he used the right waist-gun
instead of the roof-gun in the radio hatch.

Spaugh was the right-waist gunner when we had a
ten-man crew, and checked out later as a toggleer-
bombardier, when they tried to make a ground-gripper
out of him. He didn't do much of anything before the war
except go down to the beach.

Beach was the only married man on the crew. He
used to be a mechanic during the week, and a fisherman
during the week ends.

2

B-17

Crone was the armorer and the only one on the crew who knew much about bomb racks. He'd lived all over and done most everything. Sheet metal was his trade, but he'd worked in the oil fields and had been around.

Sharpe lived on a farm before the war. For a while he wanted to be a doctor, and learned a lot of medical terms and took a clinical interest in almost everything. After the war he is going back to the farm and lie under a shady tree.

Except for the bombardier and navigator, the crew was put together in the 2nd Air Force combat pool in Salt Lake City, and shipped out together for phase training and later flew a new B-17 to England.

2

TO BEGIN WITH

It was summer and there was war all over the world. There was war in Normandy and Italy and plenty of war in Russia. The same war was going on in the islands and in the sky over Japan.

The only part of the war I knew anything about personally was the air war from England. Above me on the wall was a map of Europe. Every time I came home again to England I drew another bomb on the map over the town we visited.

A good part of the time here, there is no past, and certainly no future. There is only now, the now of any oxygen mask and the now of Berlin or Kiel from 25,000 feet. That now is just as mixed up as the past, and sometimes just as beautiful.

The queer thing about this part of the war is that it never stays the same for any length of time. Sometimes it is as unreal as a dream, and as quiet and lonely as moonlight, and sometimes it is horrible and twisted with fear and the feel of death.

A lifetime is always a patchwork affair, I guess, with the seconds and hours and days thrown into a pile of other seconds and hours and days. Some of them add up into something else, and some of them are left way outside like a Fort out of formation, connected to nothing, all alone in mid-air.

I seem to be a hundred different people these days. The days take turns using the face and the body. No mood lasts more than a couple of hours. My continuity is shot.

The world is fine . . . the world is okay, maybe . . . the world is a weary hole . . . the world is a hopeless sickening mess . . . the world is blue shadows and full of sun . . . all that in a day, all that in an hour sometimes.

3
FIRST MISSION

We went on our first one on the nineteenth of April. We had a practice mission the afternoon before, the first time we'd flown in a month, and we weren't bad, so the colonel said we could go.

Some major gave us a little talk about how we might as well start sometime, and were there any questions, and just fly that baby in close and you'll come home every time.

The squadron was short on crews or we would have had some more practice missions.

After the major let us go, Sam got the crew over in the corner and told us we'd have to be on the ball from here on in.

"And you've got to fly in close," he told me. "I'm not going to do all the work."

He had slept most of the way across the Atlantic, but now he was feeling serious.

I'd only flown formation in a 17 twice, once in the

phases and once on the practice mission. I wasn't very hot.

"This is the big league now," Sam said.

Everybody said so. We'd been in the Bomb Group for four days and everyone in the Group knew he was in the big league.

After Sam let the crew go I asked him, "Are you scared?"

"I'm Sam," he said.

He was all right. He was ready to go.

We went over to the club then. It didn't seem any different. Nobody seemed to care that there was an alert on, and a raid tomorrow. Nobody went off in the corner to brood.

We had pork chops for dinner, and I sat next to a guy in our squadron named La something. I called him La French, because I could never remember the last part. He was big and acted half-drunk most of the time and he looked like a pirate.

"So you've joined our noble band," he said.

"We'll probably go tomorrow," I said.

"A joy ride," he said. "Lucky boy!"

"Where to?"

"What does it matter?" He waved his hands. "The Luftwaffe is beat. Haven't you heard?"

That was fine with me. I wanted to see a Focke-Wulf some time, but I didn't care about seeing one tomorrow.

After chow La French and I went out to say good night to his airplane. The dispersal area is way down past the skeet range and a turnip field. We took our bikes and rode through a world of blue and green and soft through the haze.

Focke-Wulf 190

We saw that the plane was chocked in good for the night, and then hung around waiting for the sun to go down.

"Sort of pretty," La French said.

I thought he was talking to himself, so I didn't say anything.

I was well established in the sack when a bunch of guys came into the room and turned the lights on. A bombardier and a navigator were putting their co-pilot to bed, but he'd broken away into my room.

He was pretty drunk, and he really had the bright stare of death in his eyes.

"So you made the team?" this co-pilot said.

I said, "I guess so." I was about half-asleep.

All he did was laugh, just stand there and laugh, until the whole room was full of it, and shaking from it.

The bombardier and navigator got him under control

then and took him away to bed. The bombardier came back after they put him away.

"That baby's got it bad," he said. "He won't last much longer. He's seen too many guys go down."

When the lights were out again I lay there for a while, not ready to go to sleep.

I wasn't scared. I was just wondering what I was doing here at all. I'd been building up to that night for a long time. I used to dream about it at school, sitting there drinking cokes with some girl, reading the airplane magazines. I used to think about it all the time in the cadets. And now we were really here, ready to go to war in the morning. We were going out to knock off the Germans.

I knew right then that I didn't know much about killing.

I didn't feel like the Polish Spitfire pilots we met in Iceland, coming over. They had it bad. They wanted to kill every German in the world. But it was different with me, I'd never been shot at, or bombed. My folks live on York Street in Denver, which is a long way from this war.

All I knew about war I got through books and movies and magazine articles, and listening to a few big wheels who came through the cadet schools to give us the low-down. It wasn't in my blood, it was all in my mind.

The whole idea was to blow up just as much Germany tomorrow as possible. From way up high, it wouldn't mean a thing to me. I wouldn't know if any women or little kids got in the way. I'd thought about it before, but that night it was close. The more I thought of it, the uglier it seemed.

What I wanted to do tomorrow was ski down Baldy up at Sun Valley, or wade out into the surf at Santa Monica, and get all knocked out in the waves, and come in and lie in the sun all afternoon.

Instead I was going on a trip, a long trip, to help some other guys beat up a town, or an oil plant, or a steel mill. It seemed like a pretty futile way to live.

Then I thought a while about the eight guys who had slept in my bed in the last four months. They were all dead or down in some German Stalag, or getting drunk in Sweden, or hiding in a French ditch somewhere. They hadn't hurt the bed much. It was a nice sack, the only good one in England up to then.

Some joker dragged me out of it at two in the morning.

"Come on," he said, "breakfast at two thirty, briefing at three thirty." It was Lieutenant Porada.

Somebody upstairs who wasn't on the list was shouting, "Drag the Luftwaffe up and give 'em a blow for me."

I walked over to the mess hall through the dark. The stars were out and it was pretty cold.

Before missions we used to eat at the big dogs' mess hall, Number 1, with the colonels and the majors, and the ground-grippers like weathermen and intelligence. I was the first one in there, and I had to eat eggs and toast for a whole hour before we went to briefing.

The briefing was in a big overgrown Nissen hut. Some major got up first an told us we were going down south to Kassel to a place called Eschwege, where the Germans had a fighter park, a sort of shipping point and comfort station for ships clearing to the forward bases. They showed us where it was on the big wall map, and how it looked to the recco cameras the last time they were over there. The weatherman showed us where the clouds would be, and the guys in charge of traffic told us how to taxi out.

The formation was all drawn up on the blackboard and I copied down all the ship numbers and where they flew. We were flying right wing off the lead ship of the high squadron.

The navigators went somewhere else for some more briefing. Sam went off to change his pants, and I queued up in the co-pilots' line for kits. The gunners were somewhere else getting the same thing. There wasn't room for them in our briefing hut.

Standing there in line, I could tell this was going to be the bad time. We were supposed to have a record escort, 47's and 51's all over, all the way. But we were going in deep, and the Germans didn't want us over there at all.

The equipment hut was a mess with everyone trying to dress in the same place at the same time. I decided to wear an electric suit because I hate long-johns. I put on my O.D.'s over that, and a summer flying suit over that and a leather jacket on top. A Mae West comes last.

I was sweating before I got into all my clothes, and by the time I had heaved my flak suit and parachute on the track I could feel the sweat rolling down my knees and pooling up in my insteps.

The rest of the crew was still struggling in the equipment

P-51 Mustang

room, so Crone and I lay down among the parachutes and looked at the stars. It was time to think again.

I said hello to Lady Luck up there somewhere in the blue. As long as she went along too I knew I'd be all right. I told her where we were going, but I think she knew already.

The others came out in time and the truck took us out to the plane. Every body was talking fast and laughing, and I felt sort of ready, like I'd been waiting for a long time for this to happen.

Lewis was trying to put his guns in the turret, while I tried to stow my flak suit under the seat where I could reach for it fast.

"Goddamn it," I said, "there ought to be more room in these goddamned things."

"Take it easy," he said.

I couldn't find my helmet, and one of my gloves was missing. Bird and Benson were all tangled up in the nose getting their guns in. Sam was the only smart one. He stayed outside talking to the crew chief until everyone else got set.

We were flying somebody else's plane, the *Keystone Mama*. I turned my flashlight on the brown lady with no brassière, painted on the side, and decided they were short of artists at this base.

Spaugh and I went up to look at the bombs, and I tore the whole back end out of my flying suit crawling through the bomb bay. We were hauling ten 500's, big and blunt-nosed and ugly things. I patted one a couple of times and it felt cold and dead.

When all the guns were in we huddled up back by the tail. It was sort of like the locker room in high school before a ball game, only not so tense.

Crone said, "I hope those bastards come in on my side."

Sharpe said, "I hope they all stay in the sack."

Beach didn't have anything to say at all. He was a sleepy guy, and older than the rest of us. For a minute he seemed closer than the others, just because he came from Denver, and we were so far from there.

I passed out the candy bars and the gum and the kits, and Sam cleared his throat.

"Okay," he said, "this is our first one. We might as well make it good."

Everyone looked all right, just a little tense, and tired of stalling around.

We started our engines at six o'clock. They kicked over right on down the line . . . start one, mesh one . . . start two . . . mesh two . . . good engines.

There was plenty of daylight when we got to take-off position. There were Forts stacked up there for blocks. They didn't look very eager, just sitting there on their tail wheels. There were a lot of new silver ones, but the majority still had the old dirty brown-green paint on, like the *Keystone Mama*.

Then we moved out on the runway, everything set, and got the green light. I watched the instruments and called off the air speed and Sam herded her down the runway. We were bouncing all over before the needle hit 120. Then Sam pulled her off, and we were airborne.

Grant gave me the heading over the interphone and we started climbing on course, away from the blood-colored dawn.

Sam and I had decided to trade off every fifteen minutes until we got used to going to war, but he flew most of the assembly, and I just changed the RPM when he called for it and sweated.

14

I thought the eighteen planes would never get together. We just flew around and around, getting nowhere, and then miraculously we were all in, flying off the right leaders, trying to look pretty.

We formed at seventeen thousand and my oxygen mask was bothering me, and my hair was soupy with sweat, and I couldn't move my shoulders in my electric suit. It was too late to do anything though.

Our group got lined up in the wing formation, but someone was off somewhere, or some other wings were way out of line, because just as I was about to sit back and look around, we went driving through into another wing on a collision course. For a few seconds there were airplanes everywhere, and we were flopping around in prop wash. Sam was screaming inside his oxygen mask, and then they were gone.

I hadn't even stopped breathing hard before it happened again.

Bird yelled over interphone, "Here they come!" I ducked and he said, "I don't wanna die this way."

Nobody got it head on, but nobody missed very far.

The air looked clear then, so Sam let me take it a while.

I held it in for a while and then started thinking about something or other, and when I came to we were way back out of formation. Sam grabbed the throttles, and I could hear him swearing into his oxygen mask.

"Get on the ball," he said a minute later. "You gotta stay in there."

Somewhere down in the formation the lead navigator was sweating out his check points, and the various squadron leaders were sweating out keeping their boys out of prop wash and in the right position, and all we had to do was hang on to that wing. But that was plenty. I was hot and my oxygen mask was trying to gag me, and I over-controlled the throttles, too much, then too little, trying to fly that big bird close.

Sam could sit there and move the throttles a quarter of an inch once in a while and keep us in tight, unless he got careless. But I just didn't have the touch. I made labor out of it. I heaved that big lady all over the sky, jockeying for position, eating up gas.

We flew up across the Channel and cut in at the Dutch coast. The navigator was on the ball, and we didn't see any flak until we were out in the Zuider Zee. Some other wing navigator was asleep and they caught it right in the middle of the formation. Nobody went down. Pretty black puffs in a blue sky . . . harmless looking stuff.

We were flying into the sun, and our top window was so dirty I couldn't see out of it at all. The front sheet of bulletproof wasn't any too clean and it war rough trying to see anything into the sun.

Bird called for the oxygen check every ten minutes. We were numbered off from the tail.

"One okay."

"Two okay," and so on up through ten in the nose. We sounded like a hot outfit.

"Fighters, three o'clock, high," came over interphone.

"They look like 47's," Bird said from the nose.

They were 47's and they hustled on by into the sun.

"We're over the Third Reich," Benson announced.

The land was all chopped up into little fields and little towns. The fields were just as green as England, greener than Illinois when we crossed it last. They used the same sun down there, and the same moon. The sky was just as blue to them as to anyone at home probably. But for some reason the people down there were Nazis.

Sam signaled me to take the throttles for a while. The

16

wing on our left was swinging in front of us, and it threw a wrench in the collective works. Everyone started chopping throttles back. I overran the lead and stayed throttles clear back too long. When I hit the power again we were faded.

I looked up into the sun and knew right then we were meat for the Luftwaffe. I could feel them up there waiting for a chance like this. I jacked up the RPM and poured on the gas and we moved back in slowly.

There were Forts everywhere, grouped into wings, winged into Air Divisions. The whole works was the 8th, Jimmy Doolittle's Air Force.

Sharpe called off some flak at seven o'clock. "Look at that stuff," he yelled. "It's all over hell."

"Take it easy on interphone," Sam yelled at him.

Maybe our wing was off, maybe everyone was off a little. Anyway, wings started swinging in for their targets in front of us, behind us, and a couple of them tried to go through our formation while we were lining up for our bomb run.

I didn't have any idea we were near the target until I saw the lead ship's bomb bays swing open.

Benson said, "We're at the I.P."

"Why didn't you tell me?" Bird said excitedly.

I thought we'd probably get left with a bomb load, but it turned out we had plenty of time for Bird to get ready to operate.

I crouched down, waiting for the flak to start. By all the rules there was supposed to be flak around us, right in our laps.

The bombs fell out of the lead ship and Bird yelled ours were gone.

"Radioman, see if all the bombs went," Sam said.

"Wahooooooooo," somebody yelled from the back end. "Look at that smoke."

Everyone was talking at once. We had the RPM jacked up, swinging off the target. Still no flak.

"We missed it all to hell," Bird said. "I couldn't even see the target."

All he had to do was toggle the bombs out when the leader let his go. Soft life.

Everyone was letting down a thousand feet so we could get out of the country a little sooner. A couple of wings off to the left were catching some flak and somebody had wiped out most of a town down to our right. We seemed to be out on the edge of the show.

"We're in France now," Benson called up. "We're out of their goddamn country."

I couldn't tell the difference. From that high I couldn't see that the people were all good guys. I did see a barn where I could hide if we had to bail out. Maybe there was a hayloft where some dark-eyed French girl was waiting with a couple of jugs of wine. Maybe there was a storm trooper with big boots and a bayonet to comb through the hay.

I decided to stay up high as long as possible.

There were quite a few airplanes in sight when we came in, but on the way out we saw thousands. Every direction up or down or sideways there were airplanes, big birds and little friends. There was one beat-up old B-24 straggling along down low with a couple of P-38's hanging around for company.

"We're over Belgium," Benson called up after a while. "That big town is Brussels."

It looked peaceful down there.

Then I remembered my flak suit stowed under the seat. It was a little late, but I put it on. Sam had climbed

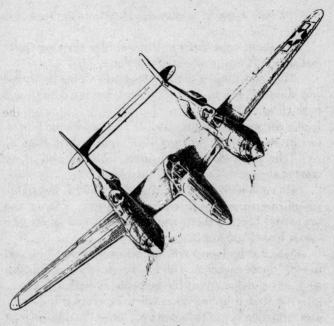

P-38 Lightning

into his, way back over the Channel, coming in. It was heavy on my neck. I flew for a while until my neck began to bend in. My neck began to ache and my shoulder was sending in sympathy pains from time to time. Then I decided it wasn't worth it and dumped the thing down in the catwalk.

Two P-51's came jazzing by, looking for game.

I traded with Sam for a while and he went on the interphone. There was nothing but shrieks with static.

Then I heard this guy call in to the wing leader, "I'm going down. Our oxygen's gone. Can you get us some escort?" He was breathing like a horse. "My navigator's

19

shot to hell. I got to go down." There was terror in his voice.

Up there somewhere in that soft blue sky a navigator was dying. It was pretty hard to believe.

The coast came in sight. Sometimes Crone or Sharpe would call off flak to the left or right, but we didn't come even close.

There were three straggling 17's down with the Liberators by then, but the fighters were herding them home.

"There's a war on down there," Sharpe said as we crossed the coast. "Look at all the blood."

He couldn't believe it and neither could I, but somewhere down there in that crazy patchwork of farms and towns and beaches there was some hard-eyed jokers who would have liked to get at us.

Sam was back on VHF. "Somebody's dying," he said to me. "Some navigator. This guy keeps calling up that his navigator is dying. What the hell good does that do?"

We started letting down when we crossed the coast. The formation began to loosen up a little. We'd heard a lot of stories about the old days, eight months ago, when the Abbeville Kids were waiting at the coast for loose formations. We stayed in.

At sixteen thousand I took off my helmet. There was a puddle of drool in my oxygen mask. I rubbed my face but it felt like a piece of fish. The candy bar tasted wonderful.

When we hit the English coast I was flying.

"Tighten it up a little," Sam said. "They said to tighten it up." He waved me in closer. "That navigator is still dying," he said thoughtfully. "That guy keeps calling in."

We were supposed to look sharp when we flew over some field at the coast, because Doolittle and Spaatz were down there watching and maybe Mr. Stettinius and Mr. Churchill were along as guests.

I don't know how we looked. I know I didn't care much. I'd never been so tired.

The navigator found the way home, and we circled the field while the low squadron peeled off.

I put the wheels down and Sam came in high and plunked us in halfway down the runway.

"We been to the war," Sharpe said.

"We're back now," Bird said.

Back on that big wide runway. We put the *Keystone Mama* back where we got her and threw all the stuff out on the ground.

"Wonder if we killed anybody?" Lewis said.

"Wonder if we hit the fighter park?" Sam said.

I was so shot I didn't want to move. My flying had been lousy. My hair was spongy with sweat and my eyes felt like they'd been sanded down and wrapped in a dry sack.

While I sat there a plane taxied by with half its tail blown off. It was one of ours. I didn't believe it.

Lewis got his guns out, and I carried one of them over and put it on the truck for him.

Sharpe said, "Well, we're not virgins any more."

"I still feel like one," Crone said. "I didn't see nothing."

We'd been there and we were home. I lay back in a pile of flak suits and closed my eyes. There weren't any holes in us, our tail wasn't blown off. Right then I didn't want to be anywhere else in the world, and these were the people I wanted to be with, these guys on this crew.

The equipment hut was jammed with guys and it smelled like a stable.

"How was it?" somebody said.

I turned around and there was the chaplain, the Catholic one.

"Milk run," I said. "A joy ride."

He smiled at me. He knew I was new. Then the smile went away.

"They got two," he said. "Two whole crews are gone."

He moved on to the next guy, but I heard someone else say they were out of the high composite.

We had put up part of another group and those guys were in the other one.

"They made a 360 at the target," somebody said, "and the 109's were up there in those clouds."

Nobody saw the fighters. They came out of the sun, and they only made one pass. One Fort blew up and one went down burning. La French was one of them and the drunk co-pilot that woke me up the night before was the other.

"That poor bastard could see it coming," somebody said.

"He knew it was his turn."

They were talking about that co-pilot.

But La French wasn't like that. He was all alive the last time I saw him. He rode that bike of his like it was Seabiscuit. And now he was just blood and little chunks of bones and meat, blown all over the sky. Or he was cooked, burned into nothing.

I thought about him all through the interrogation. I drank three cups of coffee, but I couldn't get him out of my mind.

A G.I. brought around a shot of scotch for each man on the crew. Lewis was sick and Beach was too tired, and Spaugh didn't want any.

"I don't like this goddamn English scotch," Crone said. "It don't taste like American scotch."

"I'm not in the mood." Bird pushed his away.

In the end I had a tall glass full of scotch and part of

another one. I knew what was going to happen, but I drank it and chased it with coffee.

The room got warm and the sunlight turned deep gold. La French was gone but it was no good thinking about him any more. I was there and I was alive.

Billy Behrend came along on his bike when I went outside.

"It's early," he said. "Let's go for a ride."

I didn't know him very well. He lived in the room across the hall, and he was always smiling.

We went down a road till it turned, and then we went the other way. There was a church with old gray walls and houses with thatched roofs and some little kids pulling a wagon full of milk bottles, and a muddy pond with dirty ducks in it.

There isn't any way to tell how good it was to be there. Just to be moving, just to be riding down a road on a bicycle, and breathing and laughing once in a while, not knowing where the road led to and not caring. The world was endlessly big, and so green and soft and endlessly green.

We didn't come back until late.

4
CO-PILOTS' HOUSE

Sam and I lived in the co-pilots' house. It was called the co-pilots' house for no reason at all, because there were pilots living there as well.

Sam lived on his side of the room and I lived next to the windows. There was one good-luck sack in the room and one bad. About eight guys had used one of the sacks in three months' time and one man lived in the other one all that time and eventually returned to the United States. It didn't make any difference to us. We were on the same crew.

The furniture in the room included a typewriter which was mine, a Corona, and very overworked. There was a desk with two drawers, one of which was full of letters from dames, and letters from half-mad friends, and kind friends and just friends, and a couple of people I wasn't very sure of.

On top of the desk there was a jigsaw puzzle picture of a dame with a very lovely chest, under a sheet of plexiglass, just in case we ever ran out of words while writing a letter. There was a lamp with a beat-up shade, and there was a radio for a while that somebody hooked from a sergeant a long time before. But after we lived there about a month the sergeant came and hooked it back, so we had to go across the hall to hear Sinatra.

There were two lockers and a bucket which was used as a waste basket and bucket. There was a pot to put eggs in and boil them on the electric heater, which was shorted most of the time, and which worked pretty well when it worked, boiling an egg in somewhat less than an hour, Greenwich Time.

There used to be a rather ornate light fixture hanging from the ceiling, but I was practicing my serve one day and gashed my hand, and after that we had naked light bulbs hanging from a pole.

There was a fireplace, but we never built a fire, because there were no dead limbs on any of the trees around there. There were two ugly blackout boards in the corner and they looked ugly all day. At night they fitted into the windows and stopped all the light from going out, and all air from coming in.

Above my sack, climbing, there was a picture of Margaret Sullivan with bangs, a picture of Jane Russell with legs, a picture of a little dream dame called Doris Merrick. To the left of Miss Merrick was nothing but the corner of the room, and to the right was a P-51. Then came Ingrid Bergman with her hair grown out from being Maria. Then came Ella Raines from *Yank*, and some more P-51's put there by somebody else, and some more dames, and down in the corner a startling view of Maureen O'Hara.

My field jacket usually hung on a nail and was usually dirty, thanks to me, and the cleaning outfit that pressed the dirt in good didn't help matters. There was a parachute pin on the lapel, and people used to ask if I had jumped in a parachute. Sometimes I said yes, usually no. I haven't really, but I used to lie badly sometimes. The pin was a gift from a friend who had nothing else to give.

On the door were the regulations of the post, nailed to the wood. I never read them. They were covered by two towels. I never used them. They were Sam's. On the next three nails there were (1) a washrag, (2) nothing, (3) another washrag—a pink one.

Around the top of the room, all the way around, were all the Varga girls from a Varga calendar, put out by a plumbing concern, I think. There were also a good many pictures of girls in various stages of undress and discomfort, drawn by an artist with a mischievous mind, but a modest one.

My locker was at the head of Sam's bed. On the top there was a flat piece of wood, which supported a lot of junk. There was a book by Freud and an atlas. There was a book of poems by Rilke, a book on yoga by a yogi, a Russian grammar by an Englishman, and a baseball cap from the Brooklyn Dodgers, which was blue and was sent to me by a girl who is the daughter of someone very high in that business. There was an algebra book and a couple of song sheets with the words to a lot of songs no one ever heard. There were five packages of gum which came with the room, and some sock stretchers which I brought with me, and three books by John Marquand, one bought and two borrowed. There were some lousy lemon drops and a big spoon. The ball cap was the most valuable thing in the room.

On the first shelf of my locker I kept all my shaving stuff, and some liquid to scare away trench mouth, and two three-penny bits and any half-crowns and shillings I might own. There was a bottle of after-shave which would

Colt .45

have been twice as full if someone hadn't drunk half of it after a squadron party.

On the next shelf were some shirts, a bunch of letters, and some pictures of dames I knew, and a picture of my sister getting married, and my other sister either wishing she was or asking the preacher if he would mind.

Below that were shirts and socks and probably a lot of things I heaved in there and forgot. Underneath my blouse and battle jacket on the big side of the locker there were a couple of barracks bags, a .45 and some shells, a couple of knives and some brown manila envelopes which contained letters and military documents and plots I planned on carrying through after the war.

There were always at least three shirts hanging on the door of the locker with a trench coat on top of them, and a towel or a tie on top of that, and my sick hat on the very top. On the other door, or the other half of the door, I hung my T-shirt that I wore on every mission. If you got close to it, you were sure there was a goat in the room. But there wasn't.

Sam's locker was in the other corner, and since I didn't go poking around in it unless I was hungry, I didn't know much about it. The door was usually open, and most of his stuff was on the floor most of the time. On the bottom shelf was a box where we kept our eggs.

On the door of Sam's locker there were always at least six shirts and a flying jacket, and a towel that had been used to wipe off a horse.

On top of the locker there was a picture of a girl Sam wanted to lure into marriage, maybe. Anyway, she was a dream, and some people didn't believe she was even Sam's girl. But I did.

There was a mirror on one wall, too high to get anything out of, and our gas masks were somewhere. Under the beds there were a lot of shoes. I had nine pairs, counting some claks I found in Eagle Pass, Texas, and some hacked-up G.I's I tried to make into beach sandals one night. One of the pairs of low-cuts belonged to a guy who was in Sweden, but they were worn out before he got back.

Anyway it was quite a room. There was a rug which had had ink spilled on it, and scotch and vodka, and blood, and bitters. It was a gray rug, and tired-looking.

The sacks were RAF sacks, because the whole rig used to belong to the RAF once, the whole station did. It was nice of them to let us live there, because it was probably the best room in England, even if that sergeant did take his radio back.

There were two knives stuck in the wall, and I gave one to Billy Behrend, when he switched over to fighters. He figured he might need it.

On the wall above my sack was the map with all the places I've been in Europe. Some of the towns are left out on the map, so I have to draw in the bomb in the approximate place where our formation left a big hole.

Most people in the Army could not boil eggs on an electric heater any time of night, nor lie on the sack and look at Chili Williams who was right where Sam could pat her. We were lucky to live in such a place.

England was always out the window, and I often thought I'd like to live in that room again for a while after the war, and wander around and see what the country's like in peacetime.

A DOLL NAMED AUGUST

I have spent most of my life in love with some doll or other. There was a gal named Jacquie that I kissed at a party once in the sixth grade and ever after there was almost always someone.

When I got to college it began to get rugged. First there was a girl named Rosemary and that lasted long and ended bitterly, and then there was a girl named Joyce and that didn't last long and then Rosemary came back and went out again, and then it was Nancy, and then it was Kay and maybe Phebe for a while.

So, when I went away to the cadets I had all these dolls stacked away in the past, and I used to think about each one of them when the moon or the tide or the background music was right.

Almost every gal I've known is tied up with a song. Whenever I hear *Who*, I can see Joyce in a rumble-seat, and when I whistle *Where Was I*, Rosemary walks in through the mist. If someone put a nickel in a juke box and *The One I Love Belongs to Somebody Else* comes out, if I looked around fast I'd find Nancy.

If it was windy, I'd think about Phebe with the wind in her hair and whenever I had chow mein, Kay was across the table. It gets to be hell after a while.

And when you go through the cadets and swing around the circuit from San Antonio to Sikeston, Missouri, to Independence, to Eagle Pass, there is usually some gal in town who wanders in out of the smoke. And they're all wonderful. And for a little while there might even be a chance for something to grow out of it. But as soon as that town fades out and the new life on the new station is all there is, everything fades fast. There's nothing to hang on to. You only get a few hours once a week to try to pack a whole lifetime into, and it just doesn't work, and pretty soon they are only faces, and memories without pain.

A gal like Nancy or Rosemary that I knew for a long time and talked to for endless hours, and wandered around in the night with, and went to see in the daytime, they'll probably be part of my life for the rest of my life.

Sometime, way back there before the war, I used to think about getting married, but it was more of a prayer for 1950 than anything else. I didn't have any money, or anything else, and I figure none of those gals ever really seriously kidded themselves that I'd be a good deal. Because I wouldn't. Probably all my life I'll be falling in love with somebody else. And even if I ever do get married, my wife will probably have to figure on that happening now and then. It probably won't amount to much. But there are plenty of dames in this world that suit me fine, partly . . .

So the dream is always there. Some day, somehow I'll find her, and she'll be dark and laughing and a friend of the night, or blonde with a brown face and a laugh full of starlight. And probably she is just a dream. But she is the biggest dream of them all. She is all the answers to all the questions. I suppose she is all the gals I've been in love with, and all the ones I haven't seen or met or talked to yet.

So it is a sort of a game, an endless search, and an endless quest. Only it is a lonely game, and maybe one day the loneliness will go so deep, I'll have to find someone.

When I got assigned to Sam in Salt Lake, I really began to wish for this princess to make her show. Everyone began to get the feeling then, that it was closing in, that maybe there wasn't much more time. So there was Dolly. What a neat gal she was. And there was Vee and Melba. But it was the same old deal. No time. We used up that lifetime in a week and shuttled on down to Alexandria.

Sam and I met Brooksie and Pinky the first night. And after a while there was a girl named Lois, but she wandered off with somebody else.

The pressure really began to build up there. The weather was soggy and cold, and the barracks were almost moldy with the dampness, and the flying was pretty sad after dusting around the sky in an AT-6, and the weather was knocking the schedules out, and the ground school was endless and stultifying.

I used to lie there and wonder if it was all over. Maybe I'd had my share. Maybe there wasn't ever going to be another gal for me. Maybe that part of my life was written down and tucked away in the scrapbook.

We had a place called the Silver Moon, out on the edge of Alexandria where we put in our big nights. The bartender was a kid named Joe, maybe a mulatto, maybe only quadroon, or just light-colored, and really a good guy, and together one night we dreamed up a drink with about six kinds of booze in it. We named it a Witch's

AT-6

Madness and the last thing in was green crême de menthe, and it came in a big glass and two of them would fix you up for a long, rugged evening.

Right after the Witch's Madness, this gal came along. I better call her August because that wasn't her right name, and since I'm going into her case it would be better to call her something else besides her own name.

I had two, maybe three Witch's Madnesses and when I turned around she was there. She had green eyes and she was talking about Cape Cod. She looked like the girl from the other side of the mountain to me.

"Hello," I think I said.

"Hello."

"You've got green eyes," I said. "Prettiest green eyes in this town."

I forgot what she said. She was with another guy but I got her address before things got too dim, and she said she'd go out with me the next night. She didn't. She stood me up cold. She stood me up two or three times after that. But she was always around, and she never made any excuses, she just laughed and acted like she was glad to see me, and she still looked like the girl from the other side of the mountain.

We were finishing up phase training, and everything was so knocked-out then I don't remember too much about it. All I know she was always around and I was always around, and a couple of times we had long sessions, and she told me the long sad story of her life. Every time I looked at her it was like turning a knife for the upstroke of a hara-kiri job.

She was just part of the gang. She drifted around with a lot of different guys, buddies with everyone. There wasn't any ending. We just went away on the train to the staging area.

She was there at the finish, with somebody else most of the time. I waved to her when we went by, and she yelled she'd write to me, and I figured she was probably out of my life now and a good thing too.

We staged at Grand Island, and it was worse than Alexandria. They turned us loose every night, and that meant loose. I got a taste for sparkling burgundy. We had a couple of quarts between four of us and were pretty well through them our second night there, I think it was. I looked up, and there walking across the floor was this August dame. The knife was there again. I wasn't sure it was her. I didn't see how it could be. But she came over, and it was.

"Hello," she said.

"How the hell did you get here?" I said.

34

She had come with somebody's wife. So she was there. She was with another guy then, but we danced, and somewhere halfway around the floor she told me she came to see me. "Sure," I said. "Have another big one."

"Okay," she said. "Don't believe me."

"I won't." And I didn't.

But she was around. She walked out on me a couple of times, but she always turned up again later. She was part of the gang. Part of the time we went around together.

The last night she was with me from about four in the afternoon until midnight. And we left for Europe about one o'clock. We drank some sparkling burgundy, and probably some other things, and later we went to a dance. The floor was slick, and once we went jazzing across the floor and tried to go into a tight Christiania to keep from mowing down somebody else, and the floor didn't hold. We went down on our Kazarums.

Right after that she walked out on me with another guy. Right after that we barely got back to the field in a taxi in time to warm up the big bird and take off for the northland.

Sam slept all the way, and I sat there and nursed the automatic pilot and cussed that August dame, better than she was ever cussed before in her life, probably. I really gave her hell, but there wasn't much satisfaction in it.

She was just a new kind of dame in my life. She had walked out on me so many times I was almost getting used to it. She didn't make any excuses, she just let it go and came back. She was the same with everybody else.

She didn't have anything to hold to. She was just on the drift. But she knew what she was doing. She wasn't any little grammar school bright-eyes. She had been married, and she'd lived around. I figured she was just so knocked out it didn't matter any more. And by the time I got to Iceland, I didn't care any more. When we got to England, I wrote her a letter.

We didn't get any mail for a long time, not until we went to school for a couple of weeks and were assigned to our group. Then I began to get these letters. She was down in Kansas somewhere making B-29's. She was going to be a good kid now and settle down. She'd had her big time and from now on she was strictly a worthy one. She was sorry about that night. And she was going to write a book.

". . . thinking of you tonight," she wrote me, ". . . so, thought I'd drop you a line. Thought you'd like to hear from me. I know that you don't

B-29

36

care whether you do hear from me or not, but I thought you might be a little lonesome . . . this makes four letters I've written to you and I've only heard from you once . . . isn't it tough? . . . well, I'm having quite a time with my so-called book . . . the way it is turning out I think maybe it will be just a story and then maybe it won't be anything at all . . . oh hell, I wish you were here . . . to tell me it will turn out okay . . . don't think I'll try a book until you come home and we write one together . . . won't that be wonderful? I think so. I can hardly wait, can you? Lord, never thought I'd miss anyone like I miss you. Didn't think it possible that I'd ever miss anyone, or that I couldn't get along by myself, but I'm learning that I can't. . . . When you left, G.I., it seemed as though all the fun in life had also left . . . it was so darned lonesome . . . if I had it all to do over again I can assure you things would have worked out differently . . . you know you never realize you've had a good deal until it's no longer there. I certainly would appreciate you if you were around now. Is it too late? . . . hope not . . . take good care of yourself . . . watch the watch . . ."

She was really foggy. But I could never laugh very hard about it. She was the last one. And I didn't know much about her. And when I thought about myself in connection with her, I didn't know much about myself either. Maybe we were just part of the whole big mess. A guy and a gal and a war, and probably it was happening just about the same way, with variations, all over the country. Neither of us had anyone. And we still didn't. But we wanted something.

She didn't want me much, but I was gone. And I didn't want her much, and she was gone. And for a while we were in the same setup. And then it was all gone. Really all gone.

5

AIR MEDAL

After the first two weeks it seemed like I'd been here a hundred years, and all time before that was just a dream.

We were alerted eight days straight, and we flew six missions and were called back once, and had an abortion in that time. After that first trip to Eschwege we went on a short one to Calais, and clear down to Munich on our third one. We hit an airfield just outside of Metz and flew over the Zuider Zee again to Brunswick, and swung down through the wine country around Avord to hit another airfield on our sixth.

The raids went by so fast they got all mixed up, and I couldn't remember which one came first and what happened which day. If it had kept up much longer we'd have all been so flak-happy we'd never have made it.

I was so tired of sitting in the co-pilot's seat I thought I was getting cancer of the left cheek. The cheek bone on that side was beginning to throb at high altitude, and when we got back from the ten-hour haul to Munich it was ringing like a gong, and I had to sit on half myself most of the way home.

Munich

When I was a little kid I believed the world was round, because my folks told me, And I probably heard it again in the first grade, and later in school I read about Columbus and Magellan and Sir Francis Drake and some of the early ones who went all the way round.

I suppose I believed it was all one world too, but I never thought of it that way. The map shapes were all mixed up with pieces of movies, and pictures in the roto-gravure section and the proportions were all wrong. I don't ever remember trying to think of it all in one piece, all at one time.

Then we went to Labrador. I helped Sam set up the automatic pilot, and we checked out of the U.S. and flew up north toward the Pole. Quebec unrolled and the lost lakes of the north slid under, and Labrador was there, cold and blue-white and twenty-five days by dog team from anywhere.

We fished through the ice in Labrador one afternoon, and took off that night under a brilliant show of northern lights, heading east, flying around the curve of the earth for Iceland.

A radio beam from Greenland came through on time . . . somewhere north lay the endless loneliness of the icecap . . . then the Iceland beam, and the fishing boats, and the island, dreary and fogged-in and snowless.

I thought about that trip the day we went to Munich. The formations flew down across France, through the clean sky, and four miles below the world was soft and green in the sunshine.

The Alps poked up out of the haze in the south, white and jagged and endless. The Forts turned east paralleling the mountains, heading into Germany.

I checked the RPM periodically, and kept an eye on the manifold pressure and gave the cylinder head temperature a quick once-over now and then, and kept looking away into Switzerland.

Over the top was Italy and the dusty roads of Rome. And south from there is the sea to the mined beaches of Libya and then Africa all the way to the Cape of Good Hope.

For the first time in my life I could begin to feel it all there. I sort of took the map off the wall and laid it flat at my feet.

France slopes down from those high white peaks, eases down across the Loire to the Bay of Biscay, down through the country past Paris to the Normandy coast.

Germany, too, drops down to the sea from Bavaria to the Baltic, from the high loveliness of the Tyrol to the somber horror of Hamburg and the hungry flatness of Denmark.

Somewhere up one of those high valleys was the doomed castle of the Berchtesgaden.

If we'd stayed on the same heading we'd go over the heads of the Czechs, across the Carpathians, into the land of Comrade Stalin. And if we stayed on that heading for a couple of days, taking it easy, stopping for vodka now and then, we'd still be in the land of Comrade Stalin. Nothing but Russia for several thousands of versts.

Down the other way to the right lay the vast mystery

of West China and the Himalayas, unknown, uncharted, brooding, sleeping, buried behind fear and time and the ranges of always-white mountains.

I checked the oil pressure and tuned the RPM on the money, kept sweeping the ten-to-two o'clock sky for fighters, and pushed the projection on out into the sea.

Out there was Japan, and beyond that for miles of blue time the Pacific. Swing south through the atolls and archipelagos to the land of the moon maidens and lotus blossoms, and foxholes.

Somewhere lost in all that ocean was Australia, Christmas Isle, Easter Isle, Tahiti, Oahu. They were all out there somewhere, and some day maybe I'd see them all.

And out of the currents and crosscurrents would come the yellow beaches of California growing into North America, from the lazy Mexican love songs of Ensenada to the hot and heavy power song of Detroit and Pittsburgh and Manhattan.

I've hitchhiked across it, and flown over most of it, and skied down parts of it, and been pulled over some of it in a little red wagon.

I didn't have time for South America or India or the penguins down in Antarctica, because the formation was weaving around some flak and Sam wanted 2300 RPM.

"Snap out ot it," he said. "Get your mind on this."

But I'd made it all the way round.

And someway there was a change. After that I could think of each country, each island, each continent, in its relationship with the others. One world, the land lying in the sea, and all of it, the land masses and the oceans, covered by the great shifting air masses and currents of the air ocean.

The map shapes were out of the atlas and placed where they belonged, flat and full-sized and enormous.

I kept coming back to the thought of it throughout the trip. It seemed like such a big world, one great big world, that will never be worth a goddamn as a world, until it is tied together and knitted together so it functions as one world.

Parts of the world have been floating around in the ocean, getting by alone for quite a while, but some of the other pieces haven't been doing so well.

They say Anzio was lovely once, and the terns of Ascension Island could lay their eggs where they pleased in the old days. But in the end they were moved in on. In the end the isolated parts have to give to the others or be given or take or be taken.

Some people have been dreaming of one big world for a long time and doing their best to make it come true. Willkie went all the way round in a Liberator and wrote his book. And Marco Polo wandered all the way to China, and then came back to tell about it. And the nameless hooded Jesuits sailed out across all the oceans to spread the word of a man who believed in all the people, wherever they lived, black or white or variations of yellow, sick or hurt or perfectly healthy, Aryan or not quite, with a little bit of Gypsy.

We dropped our bombs near Munich and turned off the target back for England. As deep as I could see into Germany the sky was stained with smoke from the targets, scattered around smashed and missing and burning.

Maybe boundary lines have their uses, and tariffs and visas and all the other barriers built up by men on the ground, but the air flows smoothly over all of them and from 20,000 it is pretty hard to see them or any very good reasons for them.

With a few stops for gas we could fly our B-17 over all

the little roped-off states and spheres of influence, and local districts of domination.

We could wave at the people and buzz in low and make the roofs flap in the prop wash, and pull up and do lazy eights over the town hall, or stay up at 20,000 and line up the cross hairs on the local steel mill or opera house and watch the bombs drop away.

And while the little kids waved at us their houses would topple and the lights would go out, and the bomb dust would strangle the living air.

We were going home. Home is when the props stop spinning. I looked around, very tired. From up there it all looked so green and beautiful, and what we had done so sort of horrible.

We got our first look at fighters on that Munich haul. There were ring-around-the-roses on all sides of us part of the time.

"Hell of a scramble out at nine o'clock," Crone called up.

We couldn't tell 109's from P-51's or Focke-Wulfs. We couldn't tell which side was winning or what kind went down. They looked like they were playing around, and then one broke off in a dive that ended when he hit the ground.

"Jesus!" Sharpe said. "Did you see that?"

The explosion died away to a bloody glow. Somebody was dead down there.

All the way in from the Rhine it was like that.

"Somebody just crashed down there," Sharpe said a few minutes later.

Crone said, "I saw him, looked like a P-51."

"It was an Me 109," Spaugh said positively.

"There goes another one," Spaugh said.

A few of them were getting through the fighter cover

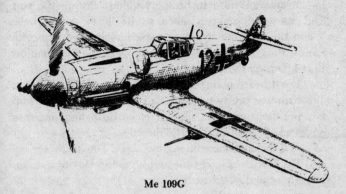

Me 109G

to the Forts. The wings ahead of us on the road in got all the business. Every few minutes we'd see a Fort peel off, maybe trailing smoke, maybe not, heading for Switzerland.

"Christ, there goes a Fort!" Sam said.

I only saw the pieces fluttering down through the straggling flame.

Another Fort pointed down into a shallow dive and never came out of it.

"Three chutes," Crone said. "I saw three."

The fighters never got to us. The 47's and 51's and 38's kept moaning over, some going home, some going up ahead for a little in-fighting.

Brunswick

We bombed through a ten-tenths undercast by Pathfinder. We flew on the left wing of E-Easy, into the sun all the way. There were bright pools of glare on both wings and I thought my eyes were going to burn up.

45

Brunswick used to be the toughest ride in the war. The 8th used to keep down its surpluses going there. When the Goering squadron moved away from Abbeville the Battling Bastards of Brunswick were the most famous Fort-killers in the Reich.

We'd heard about them clear back in the States.

Sam was pretty tense on that mission. When we were forming the squadron I slipped back a little deep once and he knocked my hands off the throttles.

"I'll fly the sonovabitch," he said. "You sit there."

He flew for a long time and he didn't look at me, and I sat there and swore at him.

When he gave it back to me, I really went to work. I wasn't smooth, and I worked myself into a lather, but I kept in pretty close. I jockeyed the throttles till I thought my left arm would fall off, but we didn't slip back any more.

We had a rough ride all the way. We were up high on the tail end of the high squadron of the high group and you work when you fly up there.

The Brunswick flak batteries got busy before we got there and threw a few acres of steel and smoke over their town.

"Keerist!" I heard Bird say softly. "Jesus Keerist!"

"How we gonna get through that?" Crone said.

The bomb bays were coming open, and we flew right into the middle of it. The Pathfinder ship found something and kicked away its bombs, ours went away after them and the formation wheeled off south into the clear.

Sam was in a good mood by the time we hit the Zuider Zee. The undercast was breaking up and we could see chunks of the Netherlands down there.

I started to take off my flak suit as we were crossing the coast.

46

"Lieutenant Newton," Sharpe called. "Don't slow down any." His voice was thin and tight. I looked back and the black puffs were tracking behind us, maybe fifty feet shy. They had the altitude and the direction zeroed, but their air speed was just a little off.

"Okay now," Sharpe called up a minute later. "I thought they had us ticketed." His voice was deep and loud again.

All the way home the 38's were wheeling over our formation. They must have been a new group, because they were coming right over the top of the formation, easy and sweet, driving out to the left for a look around, then swinging back to the right, then whipping off below somewhere, maybe to check the wooden shoe situation in Amsterdam.

Metz

We were after the Luftwaffe when we went to Metz. We carried a maximum load of fragment bombs so we could clean out the field.

I flew the bomb run, and Sam tried to watch the show out the window.

We could see the 51's peeling off to go down and strafe.

It's a long ride down to Metz, but we didn't see any fighters or flak going in or coming out. On the way home we could see the coast coming up beforehand. The clouds stopped there, leaving the Channel air clear, puffing up again on the English side.

We crossed the coast at the same place we came in.

We were sitting up there cool and silver and almost home, when the black puffs started coming up.

The Germans had wheeled in a mobile battery and they had us zeroed. I could see the dull flashes right outside the window. The ship lurched and gagged and I could hear the stuff hitting the wings. Little slivers of glass splintered around the cockpit. The right wing bucked and I looked out there and saw smoke curling out of the oil cooler.

"Number four's on fire," came over interphone, loud and scared.

"Just smoke," Spaugh said coolly. "Smoking bad, sir."

I looked down and we hadn't moved. We were standing still over France, and they were pouring it at us.

"It isn't the engine, Sam," I said. "It's the oil, I think."

The instruments were okay. We weren't losing oil pressure yet.

"Smoke means flame," Ross said excitedly.

"Flame means you blow up," Sharpe said.

"Feather number four," Sam said.

I hit the feathering button and the fuel-shut-off switch in one motion. I knocked off the mixture control and chopped the throttle, and pulled off the RPM. We just sat there while the prop windmilled a while and then feathered into a clean upright Y.

In a little while the smoke stopped.

We were across the coast. The flak behind us. Everybody was sounding off on interphone.

"I thought we'd had it," somebody said.

"I was halfway out the door."

"Anybody hurt?" Sam said. "Shut up. Anybody hurt?"

No answer.

48

"Take an oxygen check, Bird," Sam said. "Get on the ball."

No answer.

I had a swift mental shot of the whole lower half of the plexiglass shot away. Benson and Bird gone, maps gone, turret gone.

Then Grant came through cool and easy. "Everybody okay. We're all right. Little mixed up here. Everything under control now."

When the first flak burst, Bird had his feet up on the plexiglass trying to hide under his flak suit. A piece of metal came through the bottom and went on out through the top. A splinter of plexiglass clipped him in the forehead and he fell over backward.

"I thought I was already dead," he said later.

Grant thought so too. There was a little blood, and right then a little blood went all the way. His interphone yanked out, and he couldn't talk or hear.

"I could hear that reaper," Bird said. "I could see that big sickle."

Benson tried to drag him back on the catwalk so he could put a tourniquet around his neck.

"All I knew," Grant said afterward, "I had to give him first aid. I was trying like hell to remember what I learned in the Scouts, while I was trying like hell to drag him back there."

Bird finally decided he wasn't killed, and tried to get up.

"I told him if he moved I'd knock his goddamn head off," Grant said. "And, I meant it."

I kept looking out at that feathered prop.

"That's real honest-to-God battle damage," Lewis said.

"We're really hot," Sharpe called up. "Look at us, everybody."

49

But we weren't the only ones with battle damage. Two ships were down out of the formation, diving for the coast.

Someone was asking for a heading to the nearest base over interplane frequency. Some other ship from another group had two engines out and was preparing to ditch.

"That flak was magnetized," Bird said.

"Those guys throw curves," Spaugh said.

There was a jagged hole in the bullet-proof glass right in back of Sam, and the piece of flak chipped off the metal on the lower edge of the turret. One inch lower and Lewis would have caught it.

We brought the ship home all right on three engines and Sam set it in gently, and we taxied in and put the ship away for the night.

I thought the wings would be screens, but we only picked up five holes.

Another squadron was coming in. I saw the meat wagon start toward a ship taxi-ing in.

"Somebody's hurt," Sam said. "They shot a red flare on the approach."

We heard about it later.

A shell came up through the squadron navigator's table, through his map, past his nose, out the top, and burst about ten feet above the ship. A big chunk came ripping back through and smashed the pilot's knee, just clipped off the whole kneecap.

The bombardier told us. "We just went up and put a tourniquet on his leg. He didn't yell much. The co-pilot flew home okay."

One ship took three bursts almost inside the bomb bays. There were at least 250 holes in the waist and radio room when the pilot crash-landed at an RAF base. One of the waist-gunners had a stitching of wounds just above his flak suit across his throat. When they lifted him out they could see his lungs.

"He was so slippery with blood, they dropped him once," one guy told us.

He died in the night. The radioman got a chunk in his left eye that tore away most of the eyeball. The other waist-gunner lost his hand later. It was shredded.

"He just kept staring at it," this guy told us. "He'd try to shake it, and he couldn't feel anything, and he didn't seem to believe it was really his hand when he looked at it. All chewed to hell."

Avord

"We've been checked out on flak now," Sharpe said before we took off. "I'm ready to go home."

"We ain't seen no fighters," Crone said. "I gotta get a shot at one of them 109's."

"You fly this thing today," Sam said to me. "You stay in there."

He was touchy before the mission, and he'd thrown a hell of a nightmare during the night.

We crossed the French coast at 15,000 and stayed there. Half the time we didn't even wear our oxygen masks.

We didn't see any flak until after bombs-away. Then a group just above and in back of us flew right into a nest of it. I saw a Fort take a direct hit on the number three engine. The flames splashed out and licked back toward the trailing edge, and some of them went shooting up over the top turret. The pilot skidded the plane off to the left, trying to fan the flames away, and the crew began falling out the escape hatches.

"That's four," Spaugh yelled.

"There's another," Lewis said quietly. "That makes six."

The Fort swung around in a flaming one-eighty-degree turn and blew up way down below.

"Fighters out at two o'clock," Lewis said.

"Fifty-ones," somebody else said.

I was flying and Sam was looking for pretty girls down below. The fighters swung past the nose. There were quite a few of them, and they were doing some queer flying for escort pilots, just milling around out there.

The next thing I knew they were swinging in. One gray-silver job rolled over on his back and drove through, crosses up, all guns opened.

I saw the nose turret off to the right open up. It was the only one.

"Hey," I yelled, but my microphone button stuck.

They screamed through the low group, down and right from us, and they never came back.

"What happened?" Bird said. "Did somebody see something?"

"I shot at them," Sharpe called up. "They were 109's."

The one I saw was a Focke-Wulf.

Maybe there were some 51's too. It was over so fast I couldn't tell. It sort of looked like 51's chasing them.

"There was fifty," Crone said. "Fifty at least."

"I saw two," Spaugh said. "Like hell there was fifty."

"There were at least thirty," Sharpe cut in. "They sure were traveling light."

All I knew was there were plenty of them, and they were out to kill someone.

Abortion

We were so tired we didn't get up for breakfast, just stayed in the sack until the last possible minute.

In the rush to get to briefing I forgot to wear my G.I. shoes. Sam forgot his dog tags. When we got to the ship, Beach couldn't get his guns installed in the turret.

"Call the turret man," Sam yelled. "Doesn't anyone ever get anything done around here?"

There was a little oil dripping off number one engine, but the crew chief guessed it would be all right.

We were flying an old ship, one that had twenty-four missions with no engine changes. For three days we'd been flying a new airplane with big bullet-proof windows. It was supposed to be our own.

"So we get this crate today," Sam said. "Look at those goddamn windows." They weren't bullet-proof and they weren't clean.

I almost wrenched my shoulder out of joint on the primer, and started to rave slowly under my breath. There wasn't any armor plate.

We took off into a blue mist. When Benson called up to give me the heading, I had to ask for a repeat. The interphone was fuzzy. We were flying the high squadron for another group, forming over another field. We climbed out through the heavy haze. The cylinder head temperature on number one engine was way high. I opened the cowl flaps. The prop was throwing a wash of oil back on the cowling. "Number one is smoking a little," Crone called up. "We ain't on fire, are we?"

"We might be soon," I said. "Keep an eye on it."

53

There was no horizon, no sky, no England, just the soft gray mist. The group leader shot his red-green flares, and called his airplanes. The squadron leaders fired their flares and called their wing men and second-element leaders.

"My goddamned heated suit is shorted out," Sharpe said.

"Something's wrong with this oxygen in the ball," Beach said. "The indicator doesn't indicate."

The formation was lost all over that part of England, wandering around in the haze.

The fuel pressure was slowly rising. The oil temperature on number one was on the climb. Nobody salted off over interphone. The tension in the ship was growing into a threat.

"This is a sad goddamn crate," Sam said. "Why did we have to draw this sonovabitch?"

The wing started out across the Channel. Eight hours till chow time. Forty-five minutes till flak time at the Dutch coast. We were headed for Leipzig.

Number one nacelle was covered with oil now, the oil pressure had dropped five pounds, the fuel pressure was still rising slowly. The air-speed indicator froze up, and we stalled out, hanging in the blue mist. Sam punched the nose down and we came out five hundred feet below the rest of the formation.

"That was close," was all he said.

It isn't a very bright play to stall out with a maximum load.

Crone was having oxygen troubles too. "I think I got a leak," he called up. "The gauge is falling off."

The throttles wouldn't slide easy. I couldn't keep in position and stay in. Neither could Sam. There was no horizon to go by, nothing at all to go by, just mist. The oil pressure kept on falling off, and the cylinder-head temperature kept on rising.

"You tired old bastard," I said softly. I could see number one engine giving up after we got across the Zuider Zee, and number two and three throwing in the towel on the bomb run in the Leipzig flak area. I could feel the whole ship slowly coming apart. Combat fatigue.

The formation was climbing. I jacked up the RPM and turned the superchargers on full. She wasn't in the mood. We were about a mile behind and two hundred feet low, and getting more behind and further below.

Sam shoved the nose down, jerked off his oxygen mask, and swore all the way around the 180 degrees.

"We're not taking this goddamn airplane anywhere," he said.

The relief washed through the ship in a cool wave.

Maybe we'd get it today, I thought. Maybe the 190's would be waiting there. I could see the flak puffing up there, reaching for us.

None of that for us.

We never aborted before, I thought. The taste of the word was bad. Maybe we could have made it. Maybe that wagon would have held together. I was glad I wasn't Sam. I was glad I didn't have to decide.

Maybe Doolittle would be sore. Maybe Spaatz would call up and give us ten extra missions. They wanted those bombs delivered, those boys. They wanted to hear about black towers of smoke, and plumes of flame, and flattened cities.

It was just a trucking job, but that airplane didn't feel like trucking.

Grant found the field.

We could have feathered number one to make it look good, but we didn't.

The ground crew was all out there when we taxied in. The crew chief was looking at something on the ground. The squadron jeep was out there. Major MacPartlin had on his squadron CO look, ready to start chewing.

I knew what they were all thinking. No guts. A rough one, so they come home.

Nobody looked at anyone else while we unloaded our stuff. Nobody made much noise. The sun shone wanly through the mist.

"She wouldn't have took you there." The crew chief came over after he'd looked at the engines. "Number one is all through."

The crew brightened up a little then, and there was some chatter on the truck going back.

"It ain't natural, us being here this time of day," Crone said.

"Why did they give us that crate?" Sharpe said. "I thought we owned that other one, that new one."

"We will, after today," Sam said. "I'm going to tell those guys a thing or two."

He had to report up to headquarters with his story.

I felt as beat-up as if we'd gone all the way.

6

GROUNDED

We were like old men. It seemed like the sun had gone out of the world. I looked in the mirror and a haggard mask of a face stared back at me. The eyes were bright. And the veins were cleanly etched in the whites, and the pupils were distended. We were all like that.

"I'm gonna get grounded," Sam said. "They're trying to kill us off."

We'd been in the group twelve days. The first four days we did nothing. The next eight, we flew.

Grant had a thin face anyway, but by then it was like an ax. Bird was impossible to get along with. Neither of them could sleep.

I could sleep. Or maybe it was a form of death. I would stretch out in my sack and feel my muscles give way completely. There was no pleasure in it. They just went flat and lifeless. And then my nerve endings would die for a while, until Porada came to wake us up.

"Breakfast at two. Briefing at three."

He was always nice about it. Quiet and easy and insistent.

I would lie there and the glare of the light would smash back into my mind.

Somewhere in the Reich today. Somewhere in that doomed land. There was a movie named *Each Dawn I Die*. It was like that.

After I got my clothes on, and out into the night, it was better. I'd stand still and look away at the stars and ask Lady Luck to bring me back home. Just ask her. Just hoped she'd stay with me another day. One day at a time.

Taking it one day at a time we got through it. And then Sam got grounded.

"I told those sons of bitches," he said. "I told them they were trying to kill us."

"What'd they say?"

"They said they didn't have enough crews."

It was true. The day before we came in, a couple of crews went down. Our first mission La French went down, and the guy with the laugh. They were short all right.

"They can't fly us now, though," Sam laughed. "I'm sick. I told the doc I had combat nerves. I told him I saw Focke-Wulfs in my sleep. I told him I woke up every night with flak in my bed."

He did too.

One night he got up and smashed the window shut, and yelled, "Don't let those Canadians through here! For Christ's sake don't let them through here!"

The Canadians were gone in the morning. They left no footprints outside the window.

Another night he sat up in bed and yelled, "Pull it out!" About three times he yelled it, and then lay down again with a sort of sob.

I guess we crashed. I couldn't pull it out.

I didn't dream. I just blacked out.

The tiredness was a disease. It attacked the mind first, and moved out the nerves into the arms and legs and face muscles. To move at all was an intolerable effort.

On the ground Sam and I got along all right. But in the air I hated him. I couldn't fly to suit him. He couldn't fly to suit me. I never said anything, except cuss him out in my oxygen mask. I couldn't say anything. He could fly better.

One day when I slipped back out of formation, after he had snatched the throttles away and jammed them forward, I said, "Look, Sam, the only way I'm ever going to learn is to sit here and fly the goddamn thing."

We were over England. There weren't any enemy fighters reported.

"There are nine guys' lives depending on you," he yelled. "You've had time enough. Now fly this goddamn thing," and he gave them back to me.

I would have killed him then, with a gun or an ax or a knife, or anything.

But on the ground it was different.

"I was a bastard today," he said after that. "I don't know what's the matter with me."

I couldn't say anything, because he was right. There were nine other guys in that plane, and I could have killed them all any day. But I was tired, I couldn't keep my mind on staying in there. Sooner or later I'd drift back.

I think we would have all cracked up if Sam hadn't grounded himself. Doc Dougherty took one look at him and said, "For three days you sit on the ground. No practice missions, no anything, just sack-time."

"The doc is a good guy," Sam said.

"The doc is the best guy around here," Bird said

loudly. "The very best." He was very drunk, and loud, and ugly.

"We better all hit the sack," Sam said. "We go on pass tomorrow."

London

I was so shot when I got on the train I didn't look out the window until the train was halfway to London. Then I remembered I hadn't seen any of it. It was the same casually neat green England.

I thought about the towns I'd gone into on trains. Denver, Boise, Philly, the big town.

We came into King's Cross station and picked up a cab for Piccadilly.

"No Red Cross Clubs," Sam said. "I'm sick of the Army."

We were sick of pilots and airplanes, and each other when we thought about it.

Against a background of London barrage balloons, Sam looked okay to me again. I decided I could get along with him for a while.

The cab driver found us a hotel, lost in a court off St. James's Street. We lay on the green silk bedspreads of the twin beds and drank three double scotches while we waited for the ceiling to lift.

"Nice sacks," Sam said.

"Nice room," I said.

Then we were ready to wander. I lost Sam in the first place. After a while I couldn't remember the places. I tied up with a RAF bomb-aimer, in the Ritz, and we had a

Free Frenchman with us for a while after the Savoy, and a fairy tried to join in at the Dorchester. We drank scotch till the scotch was gone, and gin and rum and Pimms and port until something happened.

When I came out into the clear I was tacking up a lonesome road in bright moonlight. Cool night, steady night, with no flak, and no 109's in the clouds, because there weren't any clouds, only the barrage balloons serene in the starlight.

The girl came out the shadows, carrying a fur. Her voice was soft.

"A bit of love, Yank?"

She looked good with the moon in her hair, but I wasn't in the mood . . . not for a bit of love. I wanted all the love or none, and I knew she didn't have that much to give.

I woke up in the right sack in the right hotel, and Sam was there. It was a nice sack, soft and deep as the night itself.

Sam woke up after a while. "Let's go to church."

We stood in the corner of Westminster Abbey and watched the people come in. Nobody pushed anyone. It was quiet there, and the people came quietly.

Most of the time through the service I just looked up at the great stained windows of that timeless, candle-lit cavern, an island of peace in the heart of a city at war.

After that I didn't care where. Sam had somebody to meet. I lost myself in the streets. I watched the barges and the river boats and listened to Big Ben, and waited for Churchill to show up at Number 10 Downing for a while.

I queued up for a bus ride to somewhere, and then rode another one back. I wondered what it would be like to marry a duchess and live in a palace. Everywhere I looked there was London and more London. There were

•

61

too many uniforms, and too many Americans, and too many dirty-faced little kids. Some places were smashed, and some were only beat up a little, but all of it was new and very old and somehow strangely wonderful.

I saw a girl on the edge of a crowd that had gathered to watch a hunchback strongman tear a phone book in half. I stood beside her and laughed when she laughed and smiled when she turned.

"Pretty rugged!" I said.

She still smiled.

We had chow in a little Russian place on Oxford Street, and we drank nut-brown ale until closing time in a quiet little pub called the New Moon Arms, I think. We threw darts with some Royal Engineers and lost three times in a row.

She was a Russian and a Czech, with a little Polish and French thrown in.

"Call me Mary," she said.

It should have been something long and full of vowel sounds, but I called her Mary. Her hair hung dark and loose and her eyes were very clear and deep. She had to go to work at midnight.

I said good-by to her in the shadows, and the moonlight was full and sweet in the streets.

I was lost, but I found my way back to the sack with the green silk spread. Sam had gone. I stood outside a moment and listened to the city, London under the moon. Tomorrow it might be Berlin under the sun.

Somehow I didn't care. Everything was different now. For a while I'd been away from it.

Commando

There is a certain type of doll found in London called the Piccadilly Commando. A typical commando would be named Legion and her middle name would be Host and her last name would be Lots or Many or Thousands, and she'd probably be wearing a sable cape.

When the dusk begins to grip the streets, the commandos come out of hiding and head for their respective theaters. The top operators wander along the edges of Hyde Park and past the Grosvenor House. There are dark-eyed French girls in the eddies along Bond Street, but most of them are in and around Piccadilly.

They ease along the avenues and they're always willing to talk, sometimes for quite a while, if business is flourishing, and they think they won't lose anything by it.

You couldn't pick a typical life story. She might have been born in the south of France, or maybe in a bower of heather in the Isle of Skye. About all you can say is she was born.

Maybe her father drank flagons of ale and threw the empties at her. Maybe her mother made love with the ironmonger and didn't pull the shades. Maybe her sisters read unclean books.

If she went to school it was probably casually, and she probably spent most of her time looking out the window at the dandelions, or out behind the hedges with the little boys.

She can see in the dark, and she can hear the casual white-feet of an MP a block away.

She and her sisters come from every battered city in

Europe, and she can whisper her sales talk in a dozen languages, including Braille and Indian Sign, but she is at her best in the tongue of the Yanqui.

She is part of the night of London, part of the magic, part of the ugly loneliness. She fills in an hour or a stray ten minutes or any part of a night. She is someone, when all that is needed is someone. At least she is a human being.

She may be a hard-eyed bitch in the dawn, and she may put you away without pay for months, but when the mist is in your brain, and the war is yesterday and overhead and probably tomorrow, she is the princess of darkness.

Some day the Yanks will go home, and the bit-of-love for five pounds will deflate like the barrage balloons, and her phase of lend-lease will unofficially terminate.

Maybe she'll marry a shell-shocked tank driver who'll take her home to Detroit, or maybe a flak-happy bomb-aimer and go back to the Isle of Skye.

She might make a dutiful mother and an excellent cook. And the past might fit into the past as merely an interlude, and grow over with time, and be almost forgotten in time.

Or maybe one gentle spring morning the bobbies will fish her out of the river and no one will care whether her name was Legion or Host or Thousands, whether she plied her trade along Bond Street or in the soft shadows of Piccadilly.

A DOLL NAMED AUGUST

I got another letter from August.

". . . how are you doing," she wrote. ". . . I
got sort of lonesome for you so I thought I'd drop
you a line and let you know how much I'm
missing you . . . do you know . . . I've been
writing you every day and how often do you
write me—once a week. . . . Oh God, how I
wish you were on your way flying home to me
who has my arms outstretched waiting for you to
enter them."

She was really winding up. Right about then I would
have given plenty for some of that who-has-my-arms-out-
stretched. . . .

"Please hurry home, will you? . . . frankly,
if I'd only known I'd feel like this about you . . .

I would have appreciated you lots more than I did . . . but that's the way things go . . . you don't appreciate anything until it is out of your reach and then you want it worse than before. . . . I swear things are different now. I realize lots of things I didn't before . . . one is how fine and decent you are . . . you're a person that anyone would be proud to claim as their own. . . ."

I figured she had probably been hitting the sparkling burgundy again.

It was a funny letter, but the hell of it was, it was sort of sad too. She was a gay little girl when I knew her. Nothing mattered. And now all the boys were gone and she was building airplanes and going straight home nights and being a good little girl.

She said she was, anyway, and maybe she was. She always believed something when she said it. But when I knew her nothing she said ever came true.

But it was nice to get the letter. It picked me up a little.

7

MAC

Mac was a Phi Gam, the same as Sam and I. He went through flight training as a second lieutenant, and Sam knew him then. I met him at Alexandria. He was a good guy.

Almost from the first we were pretty close. We spent most of our time at Alexandria arguing and chasing a little doll named Lois. Lois preferred Mac.

The lucky thing seemed to be, we all wound up in the same outfit. Mac came in a couple of days after us. He took off for Labrador ahead of us, but we caught up in Iceland. We were together in school for a while down near London, and we checked out for the group.

"See you, Mac," I said then. "Some day we'll settle something."

Anywhere he was could never be dull. He was the best guy to talk to I've ever known.

When he came to the group after us, I thought the luck was really turned on.

The first thing we heard when we got back from London and signed in at the orderly room: "You know that ship you wanted?" one of the sergeants asked.

"Yeah." Sam was ready to battle for it. They'd promised it to us.

"It went down."

"Who?"

"Some guy named Mac something."

It was Mac.

After a while I went to see some of the guys who went along on that trip. It was flak, right at the coast. He was the only one who went down that day in the whole 8th Air Force. One out of a thousand.

It's sort of queer when a guy goes down. Everything goes on. You keep waiting for him to come back from a leave. In a quiet moment he just checks out. It isn't like seeing him get shot in half while you lie in the grass somewhere. It doesn't mean anything at all at first. You just say, Mac's gone, Mac went down, Mac's had it, and you don't really believe it yet.

And then you wake up some night, after you've been arguing with him in a dream. And you walk into the mess hall, and save a seat for him before you remember. It hits you slow, like cancer. It builds up inside you into something pretty grim and pretty ugly. Why did it have to be him? Why did it have to be?

For a while I was going to write to his mother. I even started a letter once. But there was nothing to say.

What can you tell a guy's mother? She was there first. She knows pretty well what was inside him. Most people don't change so much after they leave home. What's there is there, and it comes from her and his father, and the people he lived with, his brother and sisters, and the kids in the block.

I could have told her Mac was my best friend. But I wasn't anyone to her. I'd only be a name. I could have told her he was the one guy I could talk to any time and get something every time.

The guys that saw him go down said they must have got a direct hit. They sagged down through the undercast. A couple of the crew turned up in German Stalags. Mac may be working his way out of France now, may be back tomorrow.

He has plenty to come back to. He won a scholarship to Harvard law school. He wanted to help run the country. Maybe he would have turned up in the Senate some day. Mac had a mind. When he said something it usually made sense.

He could fly his airplane too. He could sock in close in formation and hold it there all day long. He never got sore and started kicking the airplane around. And he knew plenty about engines and flaps and landing gear and hydraulic systems and electrical systems. He could set up an auto-pilot the way the Honeywell Company intended.

All he lacked was luck.

"I'll stack my enlisted men against any crew in the Army," he said once. "The officers are just average, but my enlisted men are the best."

All they lacked was luck.

He could whistle a line of goods any girl enjoyed listening to. I don't know what he told that Lois, but I couldn't find anything to match it. He moved in on a little dame when we were in Grand Island, and she really went mad for him.

Maybe it was his eyes. They were clear brown, and they seemed to look inside you when he was interested. He wasn't the best-looking guy in the world, but after they saw his eyes plenty of women thought so.

Mac did a lot of bitching. He didn't think much of the condition of the world. He wasn't sure anything was going to turn out worth a damn. Stupid people drove him nuts. He wanted to get going now. He wanted to start working on the changes.

"This goddamn war," he said more than once. "This war has set me back plenty. I'd be halfway through law school by now."

He didn't even have to come to combat. He was a tactical officer at Santa Ana, and he could have stayed there the whole war.

"I just thought I wouldn't be worth a goddamn afterwards if I'd never seen what it's like," he said. "You can't tell anything about war from Balboa Beach or the Rendezvous ballroom."

In the end I threw away the letter to his mother, with nothing written below my address at the top. There was nothing I could tell her.

He was the kind of guy the world could use after the war. He had a mind, and he wanted to use it, and he was tired of stalling. Maybe he would have been a pretty big guy before he stopped. No telling.

The airplane Mac took down with him was officially ours. We flew it on three missions, and we named it the *Cool Papa*.

She was supposed to have her name painted on, while we were in London, with a picture of a dame with no clothes. A girl in the States drew up some sketches for us, and I gave them to the Group artist down at the sub-depot.

"I'll draw her on there," he said. "I ain't got no time, but I'll do it."

He was in demand.

The *Cool Papa* was Sam's name. When we were in school everyone called him cool papa, because he was such a major operator.

I wanted to name it the Witcherlybitcherly or the Nancy Moonshine and my mother wanted us to name it Colorado Colleagues, because we went to Colorado College.

Most of the crew wanted to name it after Sam's sister-in-law, Mary Helen. She came down from Omaha one night when we were in Grand Island and she is about the best-looking dame in the world.

"We ought to name it for her," Ross said.

"We ought to get a big picture of her and paste it on the side," Crone said.

"You'd always be falling out the waist window," Sharpe said.

"Cool Papa," Ross said. "That's a hell of a name. What's it mean?"

It didn't matter what it meant. The *Cool Papa* lived a short life.

The day I got back from London mostly everyone was out on a late afternoon mission. They didn't get home until nighttime. I went down to sweat them in. We had a searchlight cone over the field to help bring them to the right place. There were supposed to be three lights, but one was out permanently, and the other two were fairly casual about the whole affair. First one would take a rest, then the other. Finally, near the end they got together and crossed beams in mid-air, and looked very slim and charming.

I rode my bike down to the south light and talked to the G.I. who ran it.

"Better'n two million candle power," he said. "Big goddamn light, ain't it?"

"Big," I agreed.

"Come down some daytime," he said, "and we'll take the glass off. You can get a helluva fine tan in no time at all."

"I need one," I said. "I could use one."

The tower was sending a lot of ships around for another try that night. They were coming in four at a time on the approach, cutting each other out, floundering around in prop wash, dragging in low.

"Eager for some sack time," the lightman said. "Look, that guy ain't got no brakes."

It was a guy named Nick in our squadron.

He'd lost his brakes in the flak and he hadn't even started to slow down when he got to the end of the runway. He took out a fence and wound up two hundred yards down in some turnips. Nobody got hurt, and the plane was all right, but he beat up a good many high-class turnips.

That night there was a new moon, and every time when there was a slim silver curve of a moon low in the sky, the P-51's would be up there playing around in the moonlight.

You can wish on new moons, but a gypsy dame in New York once told me never to wish for myself on a new moon, because it would never come true, and might even boomerang and come true just the opposite.

So I'd watch the 51's and think about flying one, and think about wishing for one, and decided the gypsy dame might be right, and there would be no sense in throwing a wrench in the works when I wanted one so bad. So I'd wish the rainbows would be hitting in the Colorado River, or wish the babies in London all got enough milk tomorrow, or the dames in Orange, New Jersey, all got enough loving, and let it go at that.

When we first went into the briefing room in the morning the big wall map was covered with a white sheet. We weren't supposed to know yet. The course was all drawn out up there with a piece of yarn, with pins at the control points and fighter silhouettes pinned on where the different groups would pick us up, but we couldn't see it.

There was a way to tell approximately how far we were going before the sheet came off. Every guy coming in checked the position of the yarn pulley at the left side of the map. If the pulley was up near the top and the yarn was all used, everyone set for Berlin or Posen or Munich, and a long rugged time of it. If the pulley was way down, we were probably going to Cherbourg or Calais, and we'd be home for early chow.

The day we went to Metz, the intelligence captain pulled a fast one. He jacked the pulley up clear to the top, and everyone had visions of going to Poland, or hot flashes of a shuttle trip to Russia.

Some mornings when we came out of the equipment hut there was a black dog with white feet around the trucks. If we had to wait for the gunners, I usually hauled him over to me and scratched his stomach and rubbed his ears and wished he'd be my special buddy.

At first I just called him blackdog, but his name was Redline and he was on combat status for a while. Some captain used to take him on milk runs to France. He was okay at first, but after a while he got flak-happy in a big way and tried to jump out a waist window one day, so they grounded him, and he just came around to see the boys off in the morning after that.

Redline didn't give a damn for officers. He was an enlisted man's dog all the way. He used to let me rub his ears, but he never offered any solid friendship. He licked my hand a couple of halfway licks once or twice, but he never licked my face or nose in close.

I used to know a white setter named Barry who was cagey like Redline at first. But I broke him down, and we were comrades in time, and we used to lie in front of the fire and try to think in each other's language and tell each other how glad we were to be there.

But Redline was always a cold nose. I just didn't have it for him.

The morning before the Metz ride there was an alert on. The Luftwaffe was supposed to be sniffing around. Once in a while they sent over intruders to slip into the traffic pattern and raise a little hell. A couple of times we heard reports they did all right, coming in on ships when their guns were stowed, and blowing them up on the final approach.

The MP's came around in a jeep and told the gunners to turn out their flashlights, and the armorer to turn out the bomb-bay light. We all sat around in the dark waiting for a buzz job or a strafing party, but nothing came of it.

"It sure would be rough to get it before your wheels were up," Sharpe said. "I wouldn't want to get it that way."

Stations at four, take off at five, means there is usually a good part of an hour out at the plane with nothing to do. The gunners have to put in their guns, and oxygen has to be checked, and the bombs loaded, but the ground crews do all the work, or already have it done. There is plenty of time to think in that hour.

The first couple of missions I used to lie there and twist myself around, thinking about flak and 109's and 109's and flak and Ju 88's and rocket guns and flak and Me 410's.

That is a quick way to go nuts.

Ju 88

After that I worked out a pretty good system. I'd find a nice quiet place outside on the grass under a wing, or out behind the tail and lie down with a flak suit for a pillow.

The night before I'd copy down the words of some song I wanted to know the words to and lie out there in the mornings and whistle it a couple of times and go through the words.

I worked on *My Heart Tells Me*, and *No Love, No Nothing* and *At Last* and *This Love of Mine*. It didn't matter much what, just so it was slow and sort of low down, so I'd be thinking about some dame instead of the B-one-seven.

If I could sing like Crosby I wouldn't do anything but sing, except when I'm on oxygen. Singing in an oxygen mask is a good way to drown in your own juice.

Ceremony

Air medals come in boxes. They are sent to each squadron by the medal department of the Army which is a hard-working outfit. Whenever the boxes begin to clog up the works there is a presentation.

We got ours on Sunday.

"Everybody in Class A uniform at 1600," Sam told me at lunch.

"How come?"

"Medals," he said.

"Heroes?" I asked.

We were there, with about fifty others.

Bil Martin read off our names and lined us up in order of presentation. The air medals came first, oak leaf clusters next, enlisted men on one side, officers on the other.

We were going to have it out in the sun in front of the hangar, but it was raining. We had it in the hangar.

Engineering was running up an engine.

"Tensh-HUN!"

It was the first time I'd hit attention since I'd been in England. It didn't feel so good.

Major MacPartlin read off the citation that comes with an air medal. It is about exceptional gallantry, and cool courage under fire. I couldn't hear what he was saying because of the engine.

He read a name. The guy came forward and saluted. The major handed him his air medal and gave him a tight-lipped smile and a fast shake. They saluted each other as gallant gentlemen.

Next.

My turn pretty soon. I gave him my best salute. I think Major MacPartlin said, "Glad to have you with us." I couldn't hear because of the engine.

When I got back in line I opened up my box. It was a pretty medal. The metal part is better looking than the DFC, but the ribbon isn't. The box is blue with a thin yellow line for trim, and air medal neatly lettered.

The citation was mimeographed, with my name typed

in. The mimeograph was just about out of ink when it got to mine. The exceptional gallantry part was pretty thin.

The whole thing took about half an hour. I was looking at my medal when we were dismissed. The ranks broke up. I didn't know what to do with the box.

We were late for chow, and all the seats were taken.

Oak Leaf Cluster

The first time we went to Berlin there was a complete overcast, and the only way we knew the city lay below was by the canopy of flak they put up over the top. We didn't see a fighter that day, and none of the flak hit us.

But it was a bad day. It's always bad when you go to Berlin. On the way in the pressure was on. Coming out it eased off a little, and Sam smoked a cigarette.

When he took over again I began to think about the people down in that town. I wondered what I would have said if I could talk to them on the bomb run.

Something like: "Okay, you poor bastards, sit down there and take it. We came over here to finish off your town, and it will be simpler to start all over again out in the fields somewhere and build another one, when we're done.

"I'm up here at twenty-seven thousand and the only way I know this is Berlin is because no other town throws up this much stuff.

"I'll never know how many people I helped to kill. Sometime later, when there is a lull, I'll sit alone and wonder about that. It's an ugly thing we do to your city.

"Nobody can hand all the responsibility for this war to

you, and no country has a corner on all the sons of bitches. There are some sad apples in every land and in every town, but they never took over quite so completely anywhere, as they have in your land and in your town.

"So it has been decided to get them, no matter how long it takes. Probably a lot of nice guys will have their faces kicked in before we do, but nice guys and all are partly responsible, and there doesn't seem to be any other way.

"Some day, maybe, this senseless ugliness will stop. You'll be on your knees. And if the Frenchmen and the Poles and the Jugoslavs and Czechs have their day, there may not be many Germans left.

"But most of the people in the world are sick of killing and they will really be sick of it by then.

"So when it is over, perhaps there will be enough wisdom among the Russians and the British and the Americans to give you a way and a chance to get off your knees.

"Maybe they will have enough sense to say, okay now, we have smashed you. If we wanted to we could kill every single German in the world. You will never have another chance to conquer this world. You've tried once too often and failed for the last time. After this we'll always know what you are doing.

"So you had better look around among your people who are left, and find some leaders who can start you on the road to a someday when the other people in the world will be glad there are Germans in it too.

"Good-by for a while. We'll be back. Probably the RAF will be over tonight. And there will be other days and other nights until the horror and the hate are so deep in your streets the life will be choked out."

I wondered what they were like. They were Germans. National Socialism came to flower down there. But still, they were people. Every person in the world has some of that stuff in him.

Kiel and Paree

On the Kiel job I got my first close-up of a Fort blowing up. The flak tightened up on the group just ahead of ours, and right out at ten o'clock, not very far away, a great red wound opened up, and then the drifting pieces, and ten men and a couple of hundred thousand dollars' worth of airplane, powdered in a hundredth of a second.

And while we were watching the streamers of flame from that one, another Fort nosed over straight down and started for the ground by the shortest road. It must have dived five thousand feet, and then by some miracle it pulled out, level and into a straight-up climb. It stalled out somewhere below us, and fell off on the right wing and spun in.

"Two chutes," Sharpe called up. "There's another."

You don't remember much when the missions come fast.

The day we went to Paris the sun had a clean sweep all the way out. We came in from the west, and after I jacked the RPM up and got my flak suit set, I started looking for Maxime's and the Champs Elysées. I could see the Eiffel Tower and the river, and I could probably see almost everything else, because I got a good long look.

If anyone asks me, I can say I've been to Paris, but travel by Flying Fortress is a hell of a way to go anywhere.

No matter how bright the sun is, or how clear the air, no place is very satisfactory from four miles straight up.

And the welcome is so surly. No one is ever glad to see us.

Some day I'll have to go back to Paris and sit in a sidewalk café and wait for someone to come along who will sit and listen to my story. I'll tell him we never wanted to knock hell out of his country. We always tried to drop the bombs on Nazis exclusively. But from 20,000 a Nazi looks just like anybody else, and nobody shows up very well.

Big B

We went back to Berlin.

Coming along into the flak over the city, a Fort in a wing off to our left pitched over into a screaming dive into the flame below. The plane was on fire. All four props were turning smoothly. Maybe the pilot had a personal grudge to settle, and wanted to make sure his bombs went home . . . or maybe the pilot was a bloody pulp in his seat, and the controls were shot away, and the co-pilot was a corpse, and the plane was afraid to stay up there any longer.

The formation was pretty well broken up. We were out on our own, skirting some bad flak. We were revving up 2400 RPM and the manifold pressure was about 42 inches.

We found part of our wing on the other side.

"Fighters, way out at one o'clock high," Bird called up.

They had swung across the nose about level, and they were climbing now.

"Might be a Fort formation," he said a minute later.

They were way out there.

At first they looked like another wing of heavy bombers, strung out in a sickly straggle. But they weren't bombers. There were way too many. They were fighters.

"I never saw that many of ours," Crone said.

Some 38's cut across the nose heading for somewhere.

"Dog fight out there at three o'clock," Sharpe said.

"110 shooting at us," Crone said excitedly.

A gun opened up. Crone's.

Some 51's were rat racing around at eleven o'clock high. I was still wondering what nationality that big mob was.

It didn't take long to queue up. They trailed off out at two o'clock and came swinging in.

"Here they come," I yelled thickly.

Sam was flying. The RPM was okay. The engines were doing all right. All I had to do was sit there and

Me 110

watch them come slow-rolling through us. There was an endless stream of 109's and 190's. Some went high and some went low, and half a dozen more came streaming through us.

I don't know whether I was scared or not. Mostly I was numb.

A 190 rolled over, came straight at us, everything opened up. His gun ports were blinking yellow flashes.

He couldn't have missed us more than a few inches.

Maybe our top turret threw a burst in him. Anyway he lived one-tenth of a second more, before he crashed into a Fort in the group behind us.

All our guns were firing. The whole ship seemed to shake apart.

"My oxygen's down to fifty pounds." It was Sharpe. His voice was like a lost little kid's.

Crone crawled back with an oxygen bottle.

"Sharpe's shot in the ass," he said when he could get back on interphone. "We got a 20-millimeter through the escape hatch back here. The whole back end is full of holes."

The 190's knocked a whole squadron out behind us.

"They just went away," Sharpe said later. "This one guy crashed head on into the lead ship, and three others blew up, and the last two just disappeared."

The sky was wide and blue and empty except for Forts. Some P-51's came over, heading for Berlin.

"Right on time," Bird said. "That guy had blue eyes."

I could have counted the cylinders in his engines.

Now that they were gone we were all pretty shaky.

"They'll be back," Sam said. "Everybody get ready." His voice was high and shrill the way it always was when he was excited.

But they never came back after that one pass.

Letting down in the Channel Sharpe came up front. There was blood all over his shorts. He turned around and dropped them so we could see the wound.

"Mostly gore," he laughed.

He had a gash on the left cheek.

"Plenty good enough for a purple heart," Lewis said.

"For conspicuous gallantry and getting shot in the ass," Sharpe said. "No, thanks."

A 20-millimeter had exploded just in front of our wing and knocked out the feathering motor on number four.

Sharpe's kit was near the door, and all that was left was some powdered malted-milk tablets.

"That was what they call the Luftwaffe," Crone said. "I never even seen them till they were gone."

For a long time the Luftwaffe was in hiding, and the escort cruised around on top getting bored, and the Forts and the Libs went in and sweated out the flak and came home.

But the fighters came back, and we saw a few every day. And every night we said a little prayer for our fighter boys.

We went to Dessau, way over by Leipzig one day, and the fighters were snarled up all day long. There were brawls all over the sky. Some groups got hit, but except for a couple of shy Focke-Wulfs that strayed around our tail we didn't see any close ones.

"Every time I see a P-51, I want to go up and shake his hand," Sharpe said.

Every time they have time to queue up and come slow-rolling through, plenty of people get killed. The most hopeless feeling in the world is when you just have to sit there and wait for it, knowing you're either going to be dead in a couple of seconds, or you're still going to be one of the lucky ones, one of the breathing ones who came through it.

Day after day we were on the list, for a trip to Berlin or Nancy or Munich or somewhere. We weren't meeting any new people, or learning anything constructive, or deepening our understanding or cementing any friendships.

We just went up there and over, to knock hell out of some city with the vague hope that some day that city will be rebuilt for some people we can get along with.

Offhand it always seemed like a sort of sick way of doing things, and when the day turns up that we can start using other methods, I'm going to be one of the gladder people in the world.

A DOLL NAMED AUGUST

I kept getting letters from August. She was still making B-29's, but she was working on a deal to join the Red Cross.

One letter she wrote me started with:

". . . Oh, happy, happy day! . . . I received forms to fill out for the Red Cross and there's a chance I might hit old London yet. You can rest assured I didn't waste any time in sending them back to St. Louis. They asked me where I preferred to go so naturally I said England. Keep your fingers crossed for me, huh? . . . I've been down in the dumps lately, and as a result I didn't go to work. I don't know, I just was disgusted with myself and everybody in general. I just stayed home and played sentimental records all day and felt sorry for myself . . . then today I received a letter from you, boy if I ever appreci-

ated anything, it was this letter deal today . . .
last night was the first night I've been out and we
went to the Blue Moon which is the nicest place
in town to go to. It was a Department party and I
wasn't going at first but my Foreman told me
that I'd be the only one in the department not to
go so I went and had a lousy miserable time, four
of the girls went alone. I knew it would remind
me of the swell times we've all had at the Silver
Moon and how I first met you . . . sitting next to
me . . . oh my, to do that all over again. . . . I
swear I'll never go again . . . the girls are terrible.
They all sat and told filthy jokes to the men, men
came with some bags that weren't their wives
and they all got drunk. It was disgusting, I'll tell
you like a friend. I had two rum cokes and was
home in bed at 11:30. I'll never never go to
another of their brawls. Thank God I didn't have
a date or I'm afraid I would have had a battle on
my hands . . . well enough of this talk I'm boring
you with. . . . I think I'll send you a poem sometime . . . okay . . . well take good care of yourself and be careful . . . watch the watch. . . ."

8

BLOOD ON MY HANDS

I forget which day it was.

I was there when the ship came in. One flak shell had burst just outside the waist window. The waist-gunner wore a flak suit and a flak helmet, but they didn't help much. One chunk hit low on his forehead and clipped the top of his head off. Part of his brains sprayed around as far forward as the door into the radio room. The rest of them spilled out when the body crumpled up. The flak suit protected his heart and lungs all right, but both legs were blown off, and hung with the body, because the flying suit was tucked into electric shoes.

Nobody else on the plane was hurt. The waist looked like a jagged screen. The Fort got home okay.

I climbed in with the medico, and, getting through the door, I put my hand in a gob of blood and brains that had splattered back that way. I took one look at the body and climbed out again, careful this time where I put my hands.

I felt no nausea, just a sense of shock, just a kind of deadness inside. I walked out beside runway 25 and sat down in the grass, and watched the high squadron peel off and come in. Then I remembered the blood on my hands and wiped it off on the grass.

All the Forts got back. Nobody else was hurt. One man ran through his luck, and got it.

I didn't know the guy. The face, with nothing above the nose was too horrible to remember. The body could have come from anywhere, Seattle or Wichita or the valley of the Three Forks of the Wolf.

Maybe the guy was a quiet one who taught a Sunday-school class, maybe a dreamer waiting for a princess to dance down a moonbeam out of the sky, maybe a drunk. But now he was dead, mangled and smashed, an ugly pulp no good to anyone.

I looked away into the quiet blue of that English sky. The wind was soft through the grass, and the grass smelled sweet with spring.

Some ways maybe he was lucky . . . out in a single flash of agony, no lingering along for twenty years to rot away inside. He probably didn't scream or grovel on the cold aluminum, and slowly stiffen as the pain closed off the nerve endings. He just went away and left a useless body.

One man gone, a million more to go, maybe even a billion before this is over. Maybe everyone in the world will get it this time. There are shells enough to go around. If some efficiency expert could just figure out a way, there would never have to be another war. We could wipe out the human race this time.

The senselessness of it, and the ugliness of it, drove away all other thought for a time. Then the despair went away, leaving only doubt and a deep sadness.

In a steady endless procession, wars have swept the world, eaten away at its heart, growing from stupid little brawls with clubs and rocks to the mechanical perfection of a city flattened out in the night, so many bombs to the acre, so many planes for the job. Fill up the bomb bays and send them over, send in the ground troops to bayonet the ones who were only stunned.

It isn't quite that easy, yet, but soon . . . maybe . . .

I watched a Fort taxi past to its parking area, smooth and clean, slim and deadly and lovely, a million synchronized parts all working just for one thing . . . death.

If we could win soon . . . this month . . . or next month . . . maybe there will be a chance . . . the sooner, the more chance.

Maybe the Americans and the Russians and the English and all the others who have learned to fight together can crawl out of their Yaks and Liberators and Lancasters and General Shermans and LST's and maybe they can sit down and have a cigarette or smoke a pipe of peace.

Maybe they can go off and get good and drunk first, and make love for a while, and throw darts, and get good and hung-over.

Then maybe they can sit down somewhere, where it's quiet, and take a good long look at the whole world.

There it is, they might say, a beat-up, lousy, starving

Yak-9

world, filled with hate and manure and revenge, but for all that, look at the moonlight on the willow trees, and listen to the surf on the yellow sand, and the whisper of the wind through the aspen leaves. There is still a little hope there, and a little love and compassion. There are a few little kids without rickets and sunken eyes, and there are hollows deep in the timber where the rabbits get along anyway.

There are all kinds of people: senators and whores and barristers and bankers and dishwashers. There are Chinamen and Cockneys and Gypsies and Negroes. There are Lesbians and cornhuskers and longshoremen. There are poets and lieutenants and shortstops and prime ministers. There are Yanks and Japs and poor whites, and certain numbers of people who enjoy rape. There are Germans and Melanesians and beggars and Holy Rollers . . . there are people.

And some day we are going to catch on, that no matter where people are born, or how their eyes slant, or what their blood type, they are just people. They have legs and arms and eyes, if they are lucky, some have breasts and some have testicles.

They are not masses. They will not go on being slaves. They are just people, partly good, and partly bad, mostly balancing out. And until we call them people, and know they are people, all of them, we are going to have a sick world on our hands.

Out of the people have come St. Francis and Margaret Sullivan, Leonardo and Babe Ruth, Madame Chiang Kai-shek and Paul Robeson, Diego Rivera and Mary the Virgin, Robin Hood and Joan of Arc, William Shakespeare, and Jesus who was born of Mary in a manger. . . . And from the people have come the Pentagon Building and the totem pole, the Merritt Parkway and the Burma Road, the

Taj Mahal and the Panama Canal, the Bell Airocobra and penicillin, the Stradivarius and the prophylactic diaphragm, the birch-bark canoe and the toothbrush.

. . . And by the people, the *Song of Bernadette* and the Book of Psalms, *For Whom the Bell Tolls* and *Silent Night*, the Koran and the Lord's Prayer, *You Can't Take It With You*, and Walden, the Declaration of Independence and Magna Carta, *Tom Jones* and *Young Man with a Horn*.

And people must eat. There is wheat bread and corned beef and Haig and Haig. There is rye bread and taro root and the milk of goats. There is slivovitz and caviar and salted almonds. There is Spam and soybeans and bird's-nest soup. There is black bread with mold on it, watery soup with eyes of grease on it, and there is starvation.

They wear fur parkas and black-lace panties, ten-gallon hats and rope-soled sandals, flying suits and Harris tweeds, field boots and ski boots and cowboy boots and Levis.

Now they live in mud huts and thatch-roofed cottages, yurts and igloos and tents and caves, bombed-out cellars and moated castles. Some have bathtubs and some have the river. Some have the open fields and the rain . . . and their kids play in the mine fields.

There are factories and mines and railroads and Liberty ships and C-54's enough for the people to build a whole new world in a little while, and haul it away where they want it. They could build hospitals and sewage systems and schools and theaters and steel mills. They could prefabricate the pieces and carry them away to all the farms and dells and towns and crossroads where they are needed.

There could be tractors and portable power units all

C-54

over the map, if only the bombers would lay off, and we could agree on a way to do it.

If the peacemakers could sit quietly in comfortable chairs and look at the world and realize it has changed since the fish crawled out of the sea, and evolved into men who had to kill, because there wasn't enough to go around.

If the wise men of the United Nations could sleep in soft sacks and wake up late and eat scrambled eggs and pineapple juice and realize that if they choose, and if they take it easy and if they don't get salty and want too much at the beginning, they could work out a setup where the people of the world can feed and clothe everyone in the world, and have plenty of time left over for play.

And we could build enough schools so that everyone could go and learn to add and subtract and keep from multiplying too rapidly.

If the wise-apples could just decide now that sooner or later people will work it so that everybody has enough

92

peanut butter and toilet paper, as soon as they find the right system to work under.

If the wisenheimers could just agree that everyone should have a chance to lie in the sun and look away at the mountains once in a while, and that everyone should have a chance to shoot the moon, and reach for a star, if he doesn't raise too much hell going after it . . . to be free . . . to be responsible for his dreams to his comrades, but free to walk alone. . . .

The last of the Forts was home for the night, motors cut, wheels chocked, crews unloaded.

I sat on the grass until the moon rose, and tried to think out my own way in the world coming after, and wondered whether there would be any after for me.

I didn't know. I just wanted to live for a while and try to grow to understand some of it, just live in the world, and maybe help a little to tie it together. Maybe that waist-gunner hadn't wanted any more than that either.

I've watched some babies be born. There is always blood at a birth. There is horror and pain and the smell of the afterbirth, and the red ugliness of the new child.

Hawker Typhoon

Maybe that is the way the world is born too.

I looked away at the sky, and asked Lady Luck to fly in close on the rest of my missions, and asked that my eyes be clear, and my mind be cool.

There was hope then, and there was fear. There is always fear.

And there was love for the world, because it is a big world and there is good in it, and truth and deep loveliness.

A flight of Typhoons came over low.

It was time to be getting back. I'd missed chow as it was, and I had to wash my hands.

Incidentally

From the time I got in the cadets, lack of sleep was a problem. In England, it is a disease.

Sam probably logged more sack time in his stretch in the ETO than any other squadron of men. If we didn't fly he retired to the sack.

Some day I'm going to have a sack of my own, of my own design. It will be 12 feet in diameter, and it will be perfectly round, with a deep inner-spring mattress built to fit. I'll be able to get into it from any direction, at any angle. And right in the middle, in the softest part, there'll be a girl.

I haven't decided who the girl will be yet, but I've made up my mind about the bed.

Ball Team

In the afternoons when there was no mission we played softball sometimes, the enlisted men versus the officers. We usually cleaned them.

The field was wonderful. The infield had short grass and was fairly smooth, and the outfield was long grass, and if the sun was hot the right fielder sometimes folded up and was taking the sun among the dandelions when a fly ball came out his way.

Our club varied from fair to terrible, depending on whether we just got back from Europe or not that morning.

A navigator, named Hart, played short for a while. He was a sweet fielding-throwing infielder, and heavy with the stick. I figured he'd be about right for the Phillies when he went back, but he went down on the last ride to Leipzig.

Fletch was a beautiful place-hitter and could fill in any place on the team. I played second, and my arm was just as wretched as it ever was. I threw it out the first week, just like I always did in school, and it won't come back till next winter.

Sometimes it was so much like the old days down in Wash Park in Denver, with all the kids in the block down there. I got the feeling I was really ten years old again, and afterwards we would walk home around the lake and see if any of the fishermen had caught any carp.

Then a flight of P-51's would moan in low, or a Lancaster would circle the field to see what the score was, and I'd know it was England, and none of those guys lived across the street, and we wouldn't be playing kick-the-can in the alley tonight, and there won't be a hike to Cherry Creek Forest with the Scout troop on Saturday.

Every time we came back from a rough mission we had to shake up the line-up and twice we had to find a whole new infield. They had a hot club in our squadron once before, the best in the whole division and then they went to Schweinfurt.*

Formation

After we went on a few missions I decided if someone could figure out a simple swift way of getting a combat wing formed in the air, and on the way to the target, he could win the Legion of Merit.

Eighth Air Force allowed about an hour of every mission for flubbing around, getting the groups formed into wings. Every wing man circled around looking for his element leader, while he looked for his squadron leader, and the squadron leader tried to stay in sight of the group.

After a while they sent the leaders up fifteen minutes early to find themselves, and that helped a good deal, but it didn't cut the time any.

The Boeing B-17 is a good airplane, whether it's made by Boeing or Douglas or Vega. It's a pretty airplane too, in the air. With its wheels down, sitting on the ground, it is a lazy-looking job, with none of the eager look of an A-20 or a B-26. But once the wheels are up, and a Fort is airborne, on the way to the land of doom, there isn't a prettier airplane in the sky.

*For the full story of this raid read *Black Thursday* by Martin Caidin, another volume in the Bantam War Book Series.

B-26 Marauder

But after you've admired a Fort for its beauty, and for the way it has done its job in this theater, you can stop admiring. The Flying Fortress is no fun to fly.

If you can set up the auto-pilot and coast along alone, a Fort is a dream girl. You could have a cocktail party in the nose, and a dance in the bomb bay and it would just fly on the same heading and go on and on till the gas ran out.

Flying formation is something else. The more formation you fly the more you dream of fighters and Cubs and gliders, anything little that flies by the touch system, anything but a big heavy monster that has to be heaved around the sky.

I read an article in a magazine once containing this fragment: ". . . in this highly organized air war over Germany, where the heavy American bombers plug along in rigid formation like militarized geese . . ."

That is very nice, but the guy who wrote it is weak in the mind when it comes to heavy bombers and their formations. The word "rigid" just doesn't fit anything in the sky. The sky is fluid, and a formation is fluid.

The strange thing is, from any distance, a formation is

always static, and always beautiful. You don't hear the pilots screaming at the co-pilots and the element leaders bitching at the squadron leaders.

"Get us out of here," somebody will call up the lead ship. "We're in prop wash."

"Can you cut it down a little?"

"Can you pick it up a little? We're stalling out back here."

Bitch, bitch, bitch.

The Group leaders plead with the Wing leaders, and the Wing leaders weave in and out to stay in Division Formation, and the whole 8th Air Force gets there some way.

A ground-gripper would never notice a low squadron overrunning a lead squadron, or see the high squadron leader chop his throttles and almost pile his wing men into his trailing edges.

From the ground, or to a passenger in the air, it just looks deadly and simple and easy.

And actually it is deadly if it's flown tight, and the bomb pattern is compact, and it is simple and easy if you stay on the ball and fly. You can stay in some positions with two throttles, setting the inboard engines at a constant RPM, and moving the outboards a quarter of an inch at a time. You can fly back on the tail end of an 18-ship formation and spend the whole day sliding up on your element leader, punching rudders to keep from overrunning him, and pouring it on to catch up again.

A formation depends on its leaders. Good squadron leaders and good element leaders make formation flying easy. Bad ones make it hell.

From the day you start out in B-17's they tell you that formation flying is the secret of coming back every time.

The Luftwaffe is always looking for a mangy outfit that is strung out halfway across Germany.

When the Luftwaffe lies low for a few days, the formations begin to loosen up and string out and take it easy, then one day the 190's come moaning down out of the clouds and the whole low squadron blows up and the high squadron piles into the lead squadron, and three or four ships out of a whole group come home. After that some pretty fair formation is flown for a while.

It is always work, and nine hours of it on a Berlin trip knocks you flat, and if you have to drag out of the sack at two in the morning for another nine hours of the same thing, you feel like going over the hill with no forwarding address.

9

VOTING

There was a lot of sun in May in England. After a mission I used to shuck out of my flying clothes and take a magazine or a book and lie out in the sun and think for a while and fall asleep.

The papers and magazines were raising hell about the soldier vote all winter long.

One day, lying there, I decided to write the Governor and find out if everything was all right. So I wrote and told him I wanted to vote next November and asked him what the state of Colorado had done, and what it was going to do, if it hadn't done anything.

The next morning Tommy mailed the letter after we were halfway across the North Sea.

Some time later, a letter came in on State-of-Colorado stationery:

"DEAR SIR (it said),
    The State of Colorado has made provisions for
the soldier to vote. All you need to do is to write

to the County Clerk and ask him to send you a
ballot when they are printed.

Colorado has done its full share in this regard.
If the Government will only get the ballots over
to the boys and back, that is all we are asking.

Faithfully yours,

/S/JOHN C. VIVIAN,

/T/JOHN C. VIVIAN."

John C. Vivian was Governor of Colorado, and Mr.
Vivian at least signed the letter, and it was nice of him to
take the time.

And then I started thinking. About a month before I
went to the cadets, back in 1942, I voted in the November
elections. There was a Senate seat at stake, and a ballotful
of other business. I knew which way I wanted to vote on
the Senator, but the rest of the names didn't ring any
bells. I hadn't even heard of half the offices.

The polling place was right there in the fraternity
house, so all I had to do was roll out of the sack and go
downstairs. I looked at the ballot the lady gave me, and
then gave it back to her, unmarked, and asked her to wait a
minute, please.

I went in the phone booth and tried to call the
Sociology professor. The prof wasn't home, but his wife
was. So I asked her. It turned out she was head of some
women's league of Liberals and knew all the right people
to vote for. So I copied the names down and went back and
checked out the ballot again and voted.

After it was over I went outside and sat on the grass
for a while, and when the nausea was too much for me I went
down to Rusty's and got drunk, and forgot all about the
election until about eight o'clock at night when somebody
turned on the radio and the returns were coming in.

"You know," I kept telling people, "I voted for that joker."

Every other one I'd wave my glass around. "You know, I voted for that simple ass. Who is he?"

But the next morning it was different. The sick green sense of shame didn't go away for quite a while. A sad kind of a guy you are, I told myself that day. The first time in your life you can vote and you don't know anything about it. You don't know the people running. You don' know who backs them. A sad goddamn citizen, you are.

When I thought about it, asking the prof's wife wasn't such a bad idea. Under the circumstances it was a pretty good thing. She is an intelligent woman. She is the wife of an intelligent man whom I respect a good deal. That part of it wasn't as bad as it might have been.

But. . . .

I thought about it then, and other times later. A vote is a pretty fragile weapon. With conviction and intelligence backing it up, it can clean out a situation better than a mortar or a Long Tom or a bomb from 20,000. With ignorance and indifference standing by, it can snafu the works.

I was in Louisiana when Jimmy Davis was singing his way into the Governor's mansion, and the Long gang was raising hell in the newspapers.

I'd read about the kicking around the Negroes were taking in all the primaries.

I had thought about those things a little. But when it came to the primaries, I didn't know anything. I didn't know when, and I didn't know whether. I didn't even know the mechanics of a primary.

All the little things build up to big things. Elementary. Simple. But the complexities that grow out of evading simple responsibilities are pretty enormous.

So I gave myself hell for a while.

If I was ignorant in 1942, I'd be twice as ignorant in 1944. Only that is impossible. Ignorance is an ultimate, and I was almost ultimately ignorant in 1942.

In all the time the soldier vote has been kicking around in the news, I have never heard one single comment on it from the people who are concerned. I've lived in barracks in Eagle Pass, Texas, Salt Lake City, Alexandria, Louisiana, Grand Island, Nebraska and several somewheres in England. I have been in chow lines, bars, airplanes, and not one single time have I heard the issue even mentioned.

If I'm a sad one, I'm not alone.

It may be a little different in an infantry outfit, or a tank battalion. They would probably run a little older. A lot of Air Corps kids aren't even entitled to vote yet.

That is another thing. Old enough to fight, but not old enough to vote. Sad business.

But if they don't give a damn? I'm pretty sure they do give a damn. But it isn't a paramount with them. The big thing is, coming back. If you have to go out and drop the bombs on those people, then coming home with both legs and hands and arms is the thing that matters most.

After that the surface big things are women and liquor and sack-time. But some big things lie deep.

I don't know. I can't even guess. All I know is that they talk a lot more about God and comparatively untalked-about things than they do about voting, or being a functional part of a government, supposedly the best government so far.

And yet, in a way, I think, that is what the war is all about. Is the world for the people, or is it for some privileged coterie?

The main reason you're in a war is because you're in

103

it. As long as there is a war, you're in it . . . before it starts, before your country declares you're still in it, because that's the way wars are now.

After you're in it you begin to think about reasons. And one of the reasons thrown around these days is that people ought to run the world for the people . . . a big dream . . . but it's been around for a long time, maybe since men began to think and look around.

I've thought about it for a long time and I've decided that no matter how big the dream is, or how good it sounds, it isn't working out quite right.

How about Hague? How about Big Bill Thompson and his million dollars in that safe-deposit box? How about the plebiscites Hitler dished out to his slaves?

How about this phony campaign for President? Mr. Dewey spends a year pretending he doesn't even know there is such a job and Mr. Roosevelt comes up with the statement that he is just another soldier in the ranks. If people need him he will stay like a good soldier.

Does politics have to be as bogus as that?

Being President of the United States is just about the biggest job in the world, and the men who are being considered for the job should act like they really want it.

Sometimes I used to think about what would happen if I ever had a chance to see Mr. Roosevelt.

I suppose I'd salute first, and if he told me to sit down, I'd sit, and if he asked me what I thought, I'd try to say it as straight and true as I could make it.

I'd say, if you're President of a nation that exists for the people, and by the people, and because the people set it up that way, then you should tell them what goes on in their Government, especially in their State Department, which is supposed to be figuring out ways to get along with other peoples of other nations.

Then I'd salute, and probably get red as hell, and about face and get out of there, while my knees would still hold me.

The dream is so big . . . out of the people will come leaders, and they will be able to think, and they will be able to act, because they have grown up among the people, and they are the best we have evolved, and the most intelligent, the most tolerant, the most honorable, the most fitted. It's a long way from that . . . it is a million years from that, maybe . . . and maybe we aren't even going ahead . . . maybe we're slipping back.

The dream is so shot to hell right now. Everybody bitches about Congress, and probably Congress deserves to be bitched at and about. But those Congressmen are just what the people who sent them there deserve.

You have to be on the ball to be a citizen of a democracy that is growing up. And one that doesn't grow doesn't stay a democracy for long. Plenty of them have folded lately. A decade ago there were more: There are plenty of people around who don't believe in people, who have no faith or trust in them at all.

There is only one way. If you're going to vote at all, you have to find out what you are voting about, and whom you are voting for or against. If that is ABC stuff, then, plenty of people are weak on their ABC's. And if that is pretty simple then the law of gravity is simple too, and it always works.

. . . the P-51's came over low, and I lay there in the sun. Berlin tomorrow . . . maybe back to Big B . . . maybe back home in November.

10

TEN GUYS

We came back from Cherbourg one day. I was worn down. The flak at Cherbourg was always terrific. The formation was scattered. We had ended up at 30,000 above most of it.

We were back early though. I lay on my sack and stared at the ceiling. Sam was already asleep, muttering in a dream. I have known him quite a while. We went to school together. But I looked over there and knew I didn't really know him at all.

From the time you're a little kid, you dream about being with a bunch of guys who, by working together and just being together, give each other something that makes them more than just a bunch of guys. It makes them a team.

And somehow we didn't have it.

A great crew is just about as rare a thing as a great ball team. They just come along once in a while. There isn't much you can do about it, if you're not, I guess. It is a spontaneous thing.

We were average, better than some, lazier than most.

Take Sam. Sam is a strange kind of a guy, big and funny . . . but a lot more than just big and funny. He has a curious sort of a mind. Sometimes it is like a knife. Nothing much gets by Sam. Nobody is any faster or keener on the come-back.

But he was cloudy on some things. We never talked about the war, the way Mac and I did. We never talked about anything much, except going home, and the places we'd go first, and the girls we'd run after. I could listen to Sam tell about his big times for a thousand years, and never get tired. Some nights he would lie there for hours and just keep talking, about nights in Omaha and L.A. and Denver and the guys he used to know, and the time he and somebody did this. I'd just lie there and agree with him now and then, and he'd keep on talking. Some of the stories I've heard twenty times, but I never got tired of hearing them again.

But Sam didn't care much for war. All he lived for was to get out of it. He didn't care much for the responsibility of a crew either. He just wanted to finish up and go home. When he was in the mood he could fly with the best of them. And he knew a lot about his airplane.

Take me. I was supposed to go to fighters. I never came out of that. Somehow Sam and I never worked out very well in the air. We never got to the point where I knew what he wanted before he said anything. If I did something before he called for it, it was usually wrong. We wore on each other in the air. The strange part of it was we never carried it over to the ground. Once we got back on the ground we were okay. But he was under a hell of a strain when he flew with me, and there were times when I would have traded jobs with anyone on the crew.

So we never had a chance. Neither of us worked on it

enough to smooth it out. When we got back on the ground we were so glad to be back we didn't want to think about airplanes, so we didn't. I read a book, or beat the typewriter, and he slept or wrote to Barbara or went somewhere.

Take Grant. He probably could have been one of the hottest navigators that squadron ever had. He was smart. He was really good when he was on the ball. But he didn't give a damn about being a lead navigator. He just wanted to live, just wanted to get through and go back to running around.

You couldn't find a better guy, or a better-looking guy, slim and blond, and cool when the Luftwaffe was around. And what an ace with the women. It was sensational. We never ran around much together. When we started out we always drifted off on our own, but some day, maybe, we'll go through a town on a hot night and see what there is to do.

Take Don. He was like me, I think, with a big dream of what a crew could be. He was on a crew once before, and he idolized the pilot. There was always a certain amount of friction between him and Sam. They didn't think alike.

He knew his job. He knew that sight and he knew how to fix it, but he didn't have enough confidence to be a lead bombardier. They asked him. All he wanted was to wear an ETO ribbon with a star on it, to show he'd been in the war.

Nobody ever had such a hell of a time with his love life as Don. There was some doll in Louisiana who wrote him mad letters, and a couple at home in Oswego, and one in Texas. Then he met a little WAC in London. He was going to marry them all. The WAC was the closest, and then she went to France.

The four of us lived together in the front end of the ship, and flew about twenty missions together. The most you could say is that we came back every time. The Luftwaffe never got us, and neither did the flak operators. If we weren't a great crew we were a lucky crew. Mac might have had a great crew, and look what happened to him.

I thought about it a while. Sam sat up in bed and began to yell something about, "Get us out of here," and then he fell back down and began muttering again.

The enlisted men were different. I didn't really know what they were or could be. Lewis lived in his top turret and didn't make much noise. He was a nice guy, quiet and easy to get along with. He and Sam used to go round and round, sometimes, but I figured Lewis was a good man for any crew. He stood behind me on take-offs and landings, and when I forgot to do something he was always there, and he didn't say anything about it. He was just there. I didn't know what he could do with that turret. He'd opened up on that Focke-Wulf for one burst. He might have hit home. He was more on the ball than Benson or Bird. They didn't even start to shoot.

Lewis didn't raise much hell in the night time. He had a love back home, I guess, and he didn't drink any scotch at interrogations.

Ross was a good man to have on a crew. He knew his stuff on that radio, and he did his job. We always got along fine. It did me good just to see him grin and hear him laugh. We gave each other a steady razz about the dames. He was an operator from all the way. He spent his nights in the pursuit. He had a little blonde all lined up for me down the way, but we never got together. I didn't really know much about him, just that he was a good guy, and he had that deep desire to get closer together than the crew ever did. We kept talking about going on a party, just the crew, but we only did it once, back in the States.

In some ways I guess Beach and I were closer than any of them. We just had to think of Denver, and we were there together. He was a lot older than the others, and just a little tow-headed, sleepy-headed, slow-smiling guy. If I ever had a crew I'd want him for the ball-turret man. I don't know whether he'd be it or not, but I sure would ask him.

His wife is in Denver, so he had someone to fill up his mind, and he led a pretty quiet life on the side, I guess. Some day we're going fishing together up on the headwaters of the Colorado. He knows that country and so do I. We used to talk about it in the morning. He used to give me most of his scotch at interrogation.

If I ever wanted to start a commando outfit, I'd want Crone in it. He was the only guy on the crew who really wanted to fight. He was always bitching about not getting any shooting. He was just a little round guy, a sort of a caricature of Churchill, but I figure he was rugged. I had no way of knowing. He hadn't done anything more than any of the others, except blaze away at an Me 110 about a thousand yards out.

Crone was pretty handy with the dolls too. When we were in Grand Island he used to go around with some of the most spectacular spooks I've ever seen beaten out of the brush. They were incredible. But they suited him.

I knew Spaugh the least of all. We just grinned at each other every time and got in the ship. But he was another guy I had a lot of faith in. Just having him on the airplane helped plenty. When the crews were cut down from ten to nine men, he didn't fly for a while. But he went to work and checked out on the bomb racks and the toggle switch and came back and flew with us in the nose as the toggleer.

Any girl would be nuts to pass him up, big red-headed good-looking Carolinian. He and Crone used to travel in pairs some nights. Spaugh had more illusions, I guess. He was looking for a princess, or at least something worth while in bright daylight.

Sharpe was the one I knew best. We were on the verge of getting to know each other pretty well. He liked to use a lot of big words, and I usually knew what they meant, and I could throw some others right back at him.

He is a peace-lover at heart. He is going back to the Ozarks and retire to the shade, and some day I'm going down there and maybe we'll go fishing on the White River. He bought a cocker pup, and was playing mother pretty skillfully. He knew a lot about motherhood. He used to work around a hospital and watched a lot of operations, and learned all the medical terms for all the basic Anglo-Saxon monosyllables, and he could keep a conversation on dames on a high plane.

Up to then the enlisted men had never had to do anything more than their routine jobs. They were just the guys in the back end of the ship.

We were all in it together, but it hadn't brought us in close. We'd had an easy time of it.

In the old days before fighter cover, when the 8th was just a young outfit, crews had to grow up fast. They had to know each other, and rely on each other, and bring each other through.

Now it was mostly a matter of luck. Living through flak day after day is straight luck, not much more.

I looked over at Sam. He had on a T-shirt and a sweaty pair of shorts. He was quite a sight, sleeping away, dreaming his wild dreams.

Our crew didn't really belong in the war. We'd never really acclimated. We were just ten guys involved in a war.

I hoped the luck would hold. I asked the Lady to keep on sending it to us.

11

DREAM GIRL

The first time I saw her was just before chow in Number 2 Mess. She came in with another nurse, another Air Evac, and a flight surgeon.

We were just back from a mission, and I was turning around when she came in the door. I don't know what it was. She didn't look like any girl I ever went with, but someway she looked like all of them.

She was pretty good at it. She stood at the bar, looking like she was completely unaware she had stopped all normal activity in the room. She was just a little girl, and her nose turned up. She had green eyes and a soft tan and she was very lovely.

The sergeant came in and yelled chow was on the table, and I hung on to the last one. The three of them stood at the bar until everyone except me had left, and tagged on to the tail end.

A captain, some friend of the flight surgeon, had squeezed in on the party, next to her.

For some reason we sat down at the same table, and she was right across from me.

When I passed her the gravy she smiled at me, and when I passed her the spinach I said, "What are you?"

I knew, but I had to say something.

"Air Evac," she said. "C-47's."

"You evacuating us?"

"No. Just looking."

She had cagey eyes, pretty though. They were up here for a firsthand look at some human battle damage, so they'd know the score if they ever went to France.

It wasn't a pretty thought.

She wore brown nurse's slacks and they were made for her, and she was made for slacks. I closed my eyes and transported her into a white formal coming down the steps into the Café Rouge at the Pennsylvania. Glenn Miller would stop the band, and they'd all stand up. I'd sit there

C-47

casually pouring down champagne until she got right to the table edge, then I'd ease to my feet and bow, and steer her into her chair. We'd have some more champagne. We'd dance.

The illusion went away. They were talking about wounds of the trunk.

I passed her the lemon custard. "Put some apple butter on it." I said I did, and it looked pretty, so she did.

"Mmmm," she said.

"Yeah, mmmmm," I said.

She was just about through.

"Look," I said, "how would you like to wander tonight?"

The captain jerked like he'd been stabbed in the brisket.

"All right . . ." She was doubtful, but she was laughing.

"Who would I ask for?"

She told me.

"Okay," I said. "Wonderful, we'll go surround a few bubbles."

It was pretty fast work for me, but it had to be that way. I gave the captain a blank look and checked out.

After an afternoon in the sack I felt all right by night. I asked the other one for Sam, when I called her just before five.

"Where are we going?"

"We can throw darts, or wade in some ditch, or look at the moon or just drink," I said.

We took a cab into town and found the Kings Arms and drank.

She came from Philadelphia and the uniform came from Bonwit Teller or Saks or somewhere hot.

We talked about nothing much, about someone I knew in Philly, and someone she'd heard of in Denver.

She was engaged to a Spitfire pilot. The diamond was tastefully enormous.

When we didn't talk was the best. It was almost like being back in school, down in one of the joints, drinking during the week. She was out of the past, a sort of dream of other days, when there was woo in the moonlight, and laughter all the time.

I closed my eyes once and she was a girl named Eleanor I took to the Senior Prom in high school. It was the first time I ever jacked myself into a Tux.

"I had a hell of a time," I said.

"What?" she said.

"But it was wonderful."

I told her about it, but she couldn't understand it at all. After that we didn't talk much.

I looked at her. Her hands were steady. She wasn't having a big time, but she was getting by. Her life was mostly plasma and bedpans now. She was over here to hold the shot-to-hell boys together till they could be flown out to the operating tables in the rear. Just her being there was pretty grim.

But I could sit back and not look at her, and the flat English ale changed to a Zombie, and the smoky room became the Rainbow Roof. If there had been music it would have been Goodman, and the G.I. over in the corner humming into his glass was really Sinatra.

We went home after a while. The night was cool. The thank-you-we-had-a-swell-time was insincere. I knew I'd never be back.

Walking home in the quiet dusk, the world sank pretty low. When I reacted like that to a dame like that, it was only because something big was completely lacking.

She was pretty. She was built. She was American. So she was the past, and a halfway prayer for the future. I

116

could see her in saddle shoes and a knocked-out sweater and skirt. I could see her sucking on a coke straw, and I could see her all ruffled up after a long ride home in a rumble seat.

She was a symbol of something that was always there, in the back of the mind, or out bright in the foreground, a girl with slim brown shoulders, in a sheer white formal with a flower in her hair, dancing through the night.

12

D-DAY

We waited for so long it turned into a joke. Each time they woke us up in the night somebody would say, "It's D-day." But it never was.

And then on the sixth of June it was.

The squadron waker-upper dragged us out of the sack twenty-nine minutes after the midnight of the fifth of June.

"Breakfast at one, briefing at two," he said tiredly.

"Jesusgod," I said.

"What the hell is this?" Sam said.

We were sick of their war. We'd been in bed a half hour.

When we went to chow there was a faint glow from the moon, curtained off by a low overcast. The line men were pre-flighting the Forts, running up engines. There were a lot of RAF planes going over.

All the rank in the group made chow, tablefuls of majors and colonels and captains.

"Late bridge party," Bell said.

"Ground-gripping bastards," somebody else said. "They go to bed when we get up."

"Maybe this is D-day," I said.

Nobody laughed. It wasn't worth a laugh any more. Too many times. I drank a lot of tomato juice and hoped it would be good for the deep weariness in my knees.

Doc Dougherty was there, looking charming. "I'm going along," he said. "Maybe with you."

"See you in Moscow," I said.

Maybe it was a shuttle job. It was early enough.

The briefing map was uncovered when we came in.

France again, just south of Cherbourg.

"Good deal," Sam said. "Sack-time before lunch."

Mac, the Public Relations officer, was there in white scarf and flying clothes.

"You think this is D-day," I said.

He nodded.

The weariness was gone. For the first time I tuned in on the tension in that room. I grabbed the Doc and Bell and Sam in one handful.

"D-day," I said. "Honest to God."

They already knew.

We were in on it. We were flying in the big show.

Colonel Terry (CO), got up. ". . . this is invasion . . ." were the first words I got. There was a lot of noise. ". . . you are in support of ground troops . . ."

The excitement was a tangible thing. Everyone was leaning forward.

"Eager," somebody muttered.

That was the word, we were all eager.

The briefing officers took their turn.

". . . tanks on the beach at 0725 . . ."

". . . the troops will hit the beach at 0730 . . ."

". . . there will be 11,000 aircraft in this area . . ."

". . . you must stay on briefed course . . ."

". . . no abortions . . ."

". . . you can't go down . . . you can't turn left or right . . ."

". . . Wing says give 'em hell . . ."

". . . It'll be just like the photographs . . ."

We were bombing by squadrons, six planes. Our squadron was hitting a wireless-telephone station, five minutes before the ground boys hit the beach.

I wondered if the Nazis knew it yet. The last six raids had been France jobs. Full moon, high tide at dawn. I figured they knew.

The moon came through just before take-off time, a big yellow moon soft on the easy hills.

We formed at 17,000 in the dawn. There were Forts circling everywhere. Every two hundred feet was another layer of Forts. The sun was a deep bloody orange in the east, and the fading yellow moon lay in a violet sky.

Some of the Forts flew in combat wings and groups, but most of them were in six-ship squadrons, heading south, with a few lost ones flubbing around in the air.

The tattered overcast pulled itself together south of London, and became a steady blanket, puffed up here and there in soft cumulus.

Six-plane formations is lazy-man's stuff after big-time 60-ship wing formations. There were Forts all over the sky, pointing the same way.

We hit prop wash once, so violent I almost went out the top. Crone called up and asked us to get him down off the roof. All the ammunition in the turrets jerked out of the boxes.

"Rough," I said.

"Rugged," Sam said.

The sky was endlessly clean, with a few soapy clouds above, and the goddamn overcast below. Somewhere down there the fighters were moaning in low, beating up the shore installations. The mediums were just above them, and somewhere offshore the guys were waiting to wade in.

We could see the smoke bombs of some of the earlier groups.

"These goddamn clouds," Sharpe said.

Then just before we crossed the coast, the overcast thinned out, and I saw a curve of landing boats . . . maybe fifteen. And they were really pouring it on. The flashes of the guns were a bright stutter against the gray sea . . . and then we were over them, bomb bays coming open.

The Pathfinder ship lined up, and the bombs dropped away into nothing.

There wasn't a puff of flak in the sky, just Forts . . . endless streams of Forts all the way to hell and back.

"Step down, brother," Sharpe said. "The war's over."

The sky was a blue-white bathroom, tiled off from the war, tiled off from all the blood and hell below.

We knew they were on the beaches then, far below us, far behind. We flew on in a while, turned right and flew west a ways, and turned back for England.

We were in on it, but we missed it, curtained off by the clouds.

Ross tuned in on General Eisenhower's speech on the liaison set and told us about it afterwards.

We were all thinking about those poor bastards down on the beach. The planes would be over them, and the ships would be behind them but they had to go in alone.

"Step down, brother," Sharpe said again. "We had our turn."

Maybe we were all thinking the same thing. Our own war was over, the exclusive war of the 8th and 9th Air

Forces by day and the RAF by night. And probably nobody will ever know how much we did.

We'd be trucking the bombs over, more of them, more often, but it wasn't our own private show any more. The boys who take it the slow way had the bright lights on them now.

". . . you are in support of ground troops . . ." Colonel Terry had said.

We were all in it together now. Blood is the same whether it spills on aluminum or Normandy mud. It takes guts whether you fly a million-dollar airplane or wade in slow with a fifty-dollar rifle. But the time element is different. And we get all the breaks there.

If a German takes a pot-shot and misses a Yank on the ground, he may get another shot, and another. But the last guy that shot at us went by in a Focke-Wulf and he was four miles deep and below before I took a deep breath. The flak batteries are shooting at whole formations. There's nothing personal in it.

Maybe some of the airpower fanatics will scream that the big brains didn't give us a chance to win it our way. Maybe we could have. Maybe not.

There aren't many guys around here who mind sharing this war.

The only thing that matters is to win, and win in a way so there is never another one.

When we got home the truck didn't come for a while, so I went back behind the tail wheel and lay down in the grass.

It had been the milk run of all milk runs, no flak, no fighters, no weaving around for position on the bomb run . . . just straight in, turn right, and straight home again, alone in our blue-white world of sunshine.

The flak guns were all set low, waiting for tanks to lurch through the hedges, and jeeps to wander down the lanes.

After the truck came we got dressed fast so we could get to a radio.

We spent an empty day waiting around the radio in Fletch's room, thinking about that long shot through the clouds and the curve of landing craft.

One look was all I got. I looked out the window, south toward France and tried to imagine what it was like.

I'd been to Paris, Avord, Metz, Nancy, Le Havre, St. Dizier, Cherbourg, Calais, and all the places between. I could tell how green the fields look in Normandy. I could see no sign of a maid when we went over Orleans. I know about the sun patterns on the Seine, and the flowers in the fields, the way the Alps grow up out of the mist, east of Chalon.

I could tell, too, about the diseased sky over Paris, the flak blotches over all the towns and all the ports. If I was drunk I would probably tell about the Abbeville Kids, the yellow-nose boys of the Hermann Goering club who claimed to pick their teeth with Fortress spars. But if I told about them, I would be lying, because they were all dead or gone before I came to this theater.

I could tell about a bunch of slow-rolling 109's who lived for a while around Tours.

But none of it was very real. A Fort lives in the sky, from three to six miles up, and the only real things up there are the throttles and the feathering buttons, the engine gauges and the rudder pedals, an oxygen mask full of drool, and a relief can half full of relief.

The flak is real when it clanks on the wings, and knocks out your number one oil-cooler. The rest of the time it is only a nightmare of soft black puffs and yellow flashes outside the window.

The 190's are real enough when they swing in from one o'clock high and start blinking their landing lights. They're plenty real when the top turret opens up, and the nose guns start shooting, and the 20-millimeters blow away half the tail end of the ship.

I'd seen Sharpe in bloody shorts, wrenching his neck to see the wound on his left cheek. I'd seen what a knee looked like with the kneecap clipped away, and a waist-gunner with his brains all over the Alclad, and his legs shot off just below his flak suit. That guy was just as dead as any of those in the surf today. A dead one lies just as still in the sky as in a mud-hole.

But most of the time you don't live with death in a Fort the way they must in a ditch. The smells don't get to you, and neither do the sounds, and every night as long as the luck holds out, your sack is in the same place, ready and waiting.

I thought about those guys in the grass, moving down the roads, crawling through the brush, ready and waiting, and I hoped they made it okay.

Everything was different then, different from the day before. I wanted to get in the big bird and go over there. I hadn't been eager since I left Preflight, but I was eager then.

D-Day Plus One

It was cool in the morning and gloomy and quiet. We didn't go out. We sat around the radio in Fletch's room and listened to the King. The news afterwards was vague and no help at all.

There were a couple of carloads and new crews in for lunch, looking virginal, and they took over the mess hall completely. There was beef setting for three meals, but when I finally squeezed in at 1330 there was only weary hamburger from two days before.

I was asleep when Porada came around. "Get down to operations and we'll tell you what to do," he said.

We sat around the operations office all afternoon, waiting for the good word. The clouds were resting on the top turrets of the airplanes, but there weren't any rumors of a scrubbed mission.

Nobody did much bitching. Day before yesterday, when it was strictly an air war, we would have bitched all afternoon, and listened to the others bitch, but the war had changed: the jokers over in Normandy had priority on all bitching at that moment.

We were Hollywood stuff that afternoon. Nobody knew where we were going. Nobody cared much. The G.I.'s were beating the typewriters, filling up more filing cabinets. Danny was operating as Assistant Operations Officers must, but Captain Martin was taking it easy, as a lead Operations Officer can when he has a good assistant to do his work.

I tried to go to sleep on an egg crate and fell off and broke four eggs.

"What do you say we just sit here all afternoon," somebody said.

"It's teatime," somebody else said.

Then Porada came in with a tense look on his face and told the lead crews to get up to S2 for briefing, and the rest of us to scatter out to the ships.

We still didn't know and we still didn't care.

We took off in the late afternoon and flew to the west of England and turned south. Out of sight over there, across the Channel there was fighting on the beaches, and many dead men lay in the surf.

But we were high above all that. We had an easy one coming up. The target was an airfield, a place called Kelvin-Bastard, not so far from Lorient, where the Forts used to go in the old days.

I flew when it was my turn and watched the sun slide down through the soft blue toward the sea.

When it was time to bomb, the field was already a smoky mess from the wings up ahead. The flak started just after bombs-away.

The first four puffs were just outside the window. I could see the dull flashes as the shells burst. The formation leader banked off steeply right. The flak tracked along easily.

There was an ugly clank underneath somewhere. I knew we were hit.

Engines okay.

Instruments reading true.

Everything okay.

A helpless fear of those soft black puffs tightened inside me. It was always the same. Nothing to do but sit there and pray the luck holds.

And then we were out of it, turning toward home.

"Ball-turret to pilot," Beach called up. "We got a couple of holes in the gut."

Once you're out of it, flak never seems quite real, till the next time. The formations churn through the quiet sky, and the earth is a million miles below.

We let down in the darkening east. I leaned forward waiting for England. England! I could say in my mind, and then slow in my mouth, without moving my lips.

When I was eight years old I read *Robin Hood* the first time, and after that I must have read it twenty more times. Sherwood Forest, and Nottingham town in the days of Richard of the Lion Heart.

I used to dream of it then, waiting for the day when I'd stand at the rail of a ship watching for England to come out of the sea, out of the haze.

Almost like then.

But it wasn't the same because then England was home, more home than Colorado, more home than my folks' house on York Street can ever be.

It slipped in gently as always, clean and friendly and far off. That would be Land's End, Cornwall, and Devon. The names ring. I could sit with a map any day and say the names out loud, and never get tired of the sound of them.

Spitfire

127

. . . Torquay and Nutt's Corner and Coventry and Charing Cross.

We hit the coast at 8000 feet. A flight of Spitfires was playing in the clouds at three o'clock, low.

A guy named Mitchell lay on a cliff above the sea and watched the gulls and dreamed up the Spitfire. And a guy named Leslie Howard was Mitchell for a couple of hours' worth of movies and he crashed back there somewhere, coming home from Lisbon, probably leaning forward watching for England to show through the dusk.

Strange how any land could be so many shades of green, with the lazy netting of the lanes that wandered everywhere and nowhere. Looking down there, war was just a word without a meaning. It looked so peacefully lovely, yet the people who lived there had fought since the beginning of time, since before the Romans. And they are still fighting.

I flew my turn for a while, taking it easy, not trying to squeeze the lead ship any. I was glad when Sam took over again. It was better just to look.

I tried to imagine it as it must have been once, long before William the Conqueror, when King Lear was wandering mad on the heath. I couldn't bring it through. It didn't look like it had ever been wild. Everything looked permanent, steady till the end of time.

. . . Nissen huts, barracks, gun emplacements, airfields, . . . public houses, crossroads, bomb dumps, more airfields . . . more towns. . . .

I was so tired of sitting I wanted to bail out. Yet I would have liked to fly on for hours, up to the lands of the Scotsmen, Stornoway, Inverness, and the Isle of Skye.

Two Lancasters were landing on an east-west runway. A flight of P-51's came over the top from nine o'clock.

Though it was not my land, and though I had only

lived here a little while, I thought I knew why these quiet Englishmen raise so much hell with anyone who tries to take over.

I was tired, saggy tired, starting at the knees on up to the eyes. But I felt good, just so glad to be there, there were no words to tell it.

Not as good as after Berlin or Munich . . . but almost.

It was almost dark then, and the stars were coming through.

D-Day Plus Two

We didn't make the team. Some of the ships went down by Tours and blew up a bridge. They did a sweet job, because the tail-end planes didn't even see the bridge. It was gone before they got there.

In the afternoon Sam and I stole a jeep and went out to the ship, our new one. Roy and the ground crew had named her the *Times A-wastin'*. Sam didn't think much of the name, and it didn't strike any deep chord in me, but we figured the ground crew might as well have the honor. They took care of her and put her to bed, and fixed her up when she got scratched.

The group artist had a picture painted on it of Snuffy Smith breaking out through a newspaper with invasion headlines.

There was a secret meeting for all combat crews at three o'clock. They had to keep it secret because no one would have come if they had known what was coming.

A major got up and told us the venereal rate at this station was showing a remarkable increase.

The announcement was followed by a movie, approved by the Academy of Motion Picture Arts and Sciences. In the movie there were a lot of ugly things about sex that people never think about until they get dosed up. I was impressed for the twelfth time since I joined the Army.

Afterwards the major followed up with a short talk. The officers are just as bad as the enlisted men, he said, and the combat men are just as bad as the non-combat men.

It used to be the non-combat men got dosed up two to one, but lately only combat men have been getting passes to London.

After that somebody decided it was time we had another ball game. The enlisted men cleaned us. Some new guy caught, instead of Fletch, and he threw down to second seven times and never even came close. He had a nice wing though, if he could have cooled it off and channeled it. I got in front of one of his throws and looked around for what was left of my hand, after the ball went on through to left field.

It started to rain in the fifth inning. I had to hide my Brooklyn hat so the bill wouldn't warp. We called the game after Sam broke two bats.

We boiled some eggs when we got back to the room. I dropped one in a pair of parked shoes and spent an hour getting it out. After that I started to read an Economics book, only I'd lost my place, and I didn't want to read the whole book again just to find out where I was.

In the end I sat on my bed like a yogi and stared at Ingrid Bergman. She undoubtedly has a beautiful soul. Just looking at her for an hour was a soothing ending to a long day.

A DOLL NAMED AUGUST

August kept threatening to send me some poetry when she wrote, and the next time she did.

"Don't get eager," she wrote. "I just get in these moods sometimes . . . it doesn't mean one thing. . . ."

Then the poem started:

"I miss you, my darling
the embers burn low on the hearth
and still is the air of the household
and hushed is the voice of its mirth.

The rain splashes fast on the terrace
the winds fan the lattice moon,
and midnight hours chime out from the steeple
And I am alone.

I want you, my darling
I'm tired with threat and with care
I would nestle in silence beside you
And all but your presence forgot
In the hush of the happiness given
to those who through trusting have grown
to the fullness of love and contentness
But I am alone.

I call to you, my darling
My voice echoes back on my heart
I stretch my arms to you in longing
But they fall to my sides empty, apart.

I whisper the sweet words you taught me
The words that only we have known
Till the air of the silent night is bitter
For I am alone.

I miss you, darling,
Oh, I miss you."

I was rolled. She was turning into an Elizabeth Browning on me.

Under that she signed her name and then, ". . . didn't think I had it in me, did you, comrade?"

I didn't know whether I did or not. That dame was always a surprise to me.

13

ANY MISSION ... ANY DAY ... FOR A WHILE ...

No day ever started right that started at 0200 in the morning. We were warm in the sack, limp and dreamless, when the lights flicked on and the voice yelled, "Chow time right now. Out to the ships at 0255."

I took one egg to be cooked, and the mess operator added a pool of powdered egg and let me choose. The real egg had lived and grown old. It tasted of death.

I lay out on the ground with my chute for a pillow, waiting for the truck.

Five searchlights were coned above a field down south, slim fingers of light reaching up into the night for the RAF boys.

I didn't know where to yet. Since D-day they only briefed the lead crews. Everybody else went straight to the ships, and they brought the hot gin around with the flimsies and the candy bars.

0300. Too goddamn early.

The night was blue and lovely, and some way the

searchlights added to the beauty, so clean, reaching so high.

Then the trucks began to come for the crews.

I waited till all the chutes and flak helmets and guys were on before I moved. The truck started to move too.

Everybody yelled at the driver.

"Jack yourself on here, junior," Sharpe said.

"Rodney." British for Roger.

I couldn't see the faces but everyone was there, half-asleep and bitching about being hauled out of the sack. I lay on the floor with the escape kits under my head, and let the bumps have me.

Roy was leaning on number one prop when we got out there. White teeth smiling out through the dark.

White teeth smiled back at him. "Everything okay?"

"Everything okay. We put some relief tubes in the cockpit and the nose."

"Good deal," I said. "Good crew chief."

I threw my parachute up through the hatch first, and knocked off my earphones, climbing up after, and dropped my oxygen mask back on the concrete.

"I'll be a sad sonovabitch," I said.

"Naughty, naughty." Lewis was feeling good. "Wash your mouth out."

I heaved my chute into the co-pilot's seat and checked the oxygen supply. The fuel shut-off switches were off, off, off. Everything looked okay.

I crawled out again and went back to the tail to hand out escape kits. Sharpe was sweating and cussing his guns.

"We get any candy?" he asked.

"Maybe."

"I won't go unless we do."

"Me, either." said Crone.

The plane looked okay. Two wings, one tail, four

motors, all present and accounted for. I checked the waste gates on the superchargers and gave each tire a kick and called it a check. When Roy said a plane was okay, it was ready for the blue.

I hauled a flak suit out in the grass behind the tail. Soft pillow, soft sack.

0315. 45 minutes till engines. Nothing to do but stare at the stars and think about the flak and how tired my left cheekbone would be after I sat on it for a while.

I decided on my first song. ". . . my heart tells me this is just a fling . . ." I got the words in the right order, but there were a few quavers.

Sinatra wouldn't swoon, I decided. Then I whistled it, with tremolo, very low down. Crosby would be pleased, I decided.

I wondered how it would be to sing like Crosby. If I could sing like him, all I'd do is sing and make love and lie on the beach and get brown.

I switched over to *No Love No Nothin'*. I slipped up where it goes, ". . . my heart's on strike . . ."

"Maybe if you'd sing to those bastards, they'd give up," Sharpe said.

"Think they would?" I asked the North Star, ignoring Sharpe.

I tried *Summertime*, very slow. When I came to the part about the fish jumping, I stopped.

At home the rainbows were hitting in the little feeder creeks up high, and the ice was going out in the lakes, and the cutthroats were all red and beautiful, getting ready for an egg-rolling.

"Nothing as beautiful as a cutthroat trout," I told Sharpe.

"How about Lamar?"

"He heard me," I said to the hunk of moon. "He heard me say nothing is that beautiful in the world."

Then the squadron jeep jerked in and stopped with its lights right in my eyes. Lieutenant Porada with flimsies.

"Where to?" I said.

"Calais."

"Candy?" I held out my hand.

"Didn't your mother ever feed you?"

"We won't go without our candy."

He passed over nine candy bars and nine packages of doublemint.

"Take it cool." He was off for the next plane.

I started with Sharpe and passed them out, poking into the bomb bay for a look at the bombs.

Big ugly dead things. They just lay there. They only come alive long enough to kill everybody around. Two-thousand pounders. We go over four miles high, and let them go, and haven't the faintest idea what happens when they connect. Does the earth break in half? Does the sun shatter the sky, and do the leaves wither? I come from a land where bombs never fell. The Jerries have never slipped in at night to give us a taste of the real thing. We just didn't know anything about it.

"What a hell of a life a bomb leads," I said to Ross.

"How about us?" Crone said.

"You nervous in the Service?" Ross asked. "You get paid, don't you?"

I looked at the bombs again, and squeezed on through along the catwalk up into the cockpit.

The first soft cream of morning was filling up the sky. 0355. Time to wind the props.

There were decks of clouds all the way up to altitude, layers of dim caverns, each a sort of lost world all its own. You get the feeling that a witch on a broom wouldn't be out of place when the sky is like that, and there may be a bunch of harpies behind the next cloud.

Then some of the red-gold of the early sun spilled through. I figured heaven was the next floor up.

If people wear oxygen masks in heaven, here is one joker who doesn't want to go.

The heater went out in the cockpit and I had to fly with gloves on.

"Hey," I said to Sam, "are you cold?"

"No. I'm Sam."

He'd said it a thousand times before, but I always laughed.

The Forts wandered around the sunshine, and drifted into formation and headed off for Calais.

Since the invasion, the tension was gone.

We just flew over there. The formation was pretty loose when the togglers flip-switched the bombs out. They didn't look deadly at all, curving away into the soup.

There was a mangy fur of flak off at two o'clock low. None of it tried to wrap around us.

We let down into a hazy level of con-trails from the groups up ahead. The planes poured vapor off their nacelles and as we turned I could look back into a sort of dream world of white plumes, lovely long tails, trailing deep.

But back in that sunny whiteness there were some 109's. Sharpe called them at three o'clock low, going into the clouds.

They were back there.

"I see them babies," Crone said. "There comes the P-51's." He gave us a blow by blow account of a rat race at four o'clock low.

The 51's had jumped somebody, and there were more 51's moaning from all directions. It had been a long time since there was any scrapping in that part of the country.

Instead of breaking up the formation and letting down on instruments the group leader called that he'd nose around for a hole, and we'd all go home together, like friends.

Reality went away on a rolling drunk when we let down through the clouds, in a big hole. The sun sifted through, and there were rainbows and all sorts of mysterious dead ends.

If I could have, I would have stayed up there, just climbed out and slid off the wing and gone wandering down some of those murky passages. I had the feeling Loki was around there somewhere, and maybe some dusky princess with brown skin and dark eyes covered with mist and pale sun.

Then we broke through, and the low level was just as endless as cream puffs. Sam eased out a little from the element and dived down into one and pulled up and laughed like a circus clown.

The rest of the airplanes were good and flew along with the boss.

The senseless patternless loveliness of England showed through the holes, and I didn't want to go home at all.

But we went home. The Forts taxied in, looking stuffy and important. The MP's and the guards waved to us languidly.

There wasn't any interrogation.

After chow I picked up my bike and started out. I didn't care where. The road I took wandered around one of the dispersal areas, where the ground crews were putting the Forts away for the afternoon, up past a big barn and down through some fields.

A swallow came by on the deck and chandelled up over some high weeds. Some day I'll have to get a swallow to check me out. A B-17 just doesn't have it, compared to a swallow.

The road ended at a gate. The grass on the other side was deep; I'd been there before. The two horses were down in the far corner having late chow. I left the bike and climbed the gate, and somewhere out in the middle of the grass I sank down and lay flat on my back and looked at the sky.

The air was fresh and windy-clean and the blue faded deep into forever.

Every time I went out there I'd get a feeling of intense awareness of being alive. For a little while, whenever I was there, everything was simple. The only thing that mattered was to keep on living.

I didn't miss anything. I didn't want anything . . . and at the same time I missed everything, I wanted everything. Everything was there. I don't know what I mean, exactly, except I was never mixed up out there, but nothing was clear.

I rolled over and lay with my face in the grass for a while. When I sat up the horses were standing close by, looking at me, big and red and fat.

I had part of a candy bar in my pocket. I'd tried gum and lemon drops before. They liked sugar, and candy got by.

I held out the chocolate.

No dice with the first one.

Then the one with the white left foot came forward and took his dessert. He took it all.

Everything was still. It was a little like having your foot go to sleep, only this was all over.

I patted the horses a while, until they got bored and went back to the corner.

There was an alert on.

I went back then because we would probably be getting up for another two-o'clock briefing.

A DOLL NAMED AUGUST

August kept on writing. She was better than anyone else. Apparently she was still being a good little girl.

She copied down the words to a couple of songs and sent them to me. I didn't remember the songs and thought they were more of her poetry. I read one of them to Thompson and he sang it for me, and right after that Crosby came on and sang it for me.

Then she sent me the same words to the same song twice.

Right after that she sent me this:

WHY DO I LOVE YOU?

I love you not only for what you are but for what I am when
*   I'm with you*
I love you not only for what you have made yourself but for
*   what you are making of me*
I love you for ignoring the possibilities of the fool in me and

for laying firm hold of the possibilities of the good in me.
Why do I love you?
I love you for closing your eyes to the discord in me and for
*   adding to the music in me by worshipful listening.*
I love you because you are helping me to make of the lumbers
*   of my life not a tavern but a temple.*
And the words of my every day not a reproach but a song
I love you because you have done more than any creed to
*   make me happy.*
You have done it without a word, without a touch, without a
*   sign,*
You have done it by being yourself
Perhaps after all that is what love is.

Maybe she hooked that from someone. Anyway I'd never read it before and neither had Thompson.

She didn't wise off any more when she sent the stuff. She just wrote it down and left the comment to me.

And I wasn't sure enough myself to make any. She always had me baffled.

14

NEW ORDER

D-day was back there grown over with time.

Porada came around at 0100 on a false alarm. We got everything out to the planes and they called it off. A rumor went around that we would have gone to Hanover, bombing from 6000 plus or minus 500.

The flak artists of Cherbourg all washed out of school at Hanover. To go over that town at 6500 would be about as sane as trying to roller-skate down the Washington Monument, sober.

The rumors in our outfit were always lush. Every hangar and house and barracks and latrine on the base is wired for sound, and if there was anything coming off, somebody at the heartstrings let me know about it.

Just after noon chow, the loud-speakers boomed out with: "There will be distinguished guests on this field this afternoon. Class-A uniform will be worn until further notice."

The word got around that the four-star boys were on

hand: General Marshall and General Arnold, with friends, General Doolittle and General Spaatz.

We knew we'd be going out if all that rank was on hand.

Some time deep in the afternoon the jeeps hit the road and the squadron warning-men went out with the word to get to the ships on the double.

I was halfway into my clothes when Sam casually announced that I was staying home.

"Oates is going," he said. "You can sack."

"Oates is going?" I said. "I can sack?"

"They're going to give him a crew," Sam said. His went down. "But he has to fly a few more missions first."

Any other day that news would have suited me fine. But I wanted to taxi out by General Marshall and wave casually, like it was nothing at all, and I could do this every day with my eyes closed and my hands tied behind me, and grin at General Arnold and say hello-Boss-how-we-doing, under my breath. And also I figured it might be clear in France for a change, and I might see a tank crushing a cow, or a French girl waving, or a couple of Yanks capturing a town.

But they left me.

"I am sad," Sharpe said.

"You know what you can do," I said. "You can take a flying one at a rolling one."

I went back to my sack.

At 1930 hours I woke up with the cold thought, maybe they went to Hanover at 6000 plus or minus 500 after all.

It was too late for chow. About 2000 I went down to the Red Cross and drank tea for an hour and talked to Greta, and went through a couple of waffles.

Some guy in there said the formation was due back

around 2230. They could never have driven to Hanover in that time, so I decided they probably went to France again, and had another waffle.

With the fork in mid-air I decided it didn't matter where they went, they might run into trouble. If any one plane in the sky gets it, if you know the guys in the plane, it is a rough day in the ETO.

There was nothing else to do, so I went down by the control tower and waited for the boys to come home.

The meat wagons were down there.

I lay there on the grass and watched the blue deepen. Everything was so easy and peaceful. If I didn't look around at the ambulances it took a lot of faith to believe the war was still on.

Then I thought about Sharpe back there in the tail. Maybe a 109 was sitting up on top of a cumulo-nimbus just waiting for him to come along.

Then I began to wonder how Oates was doing. There was no use wondering about that. I knew he was doing fine. I decided Sam would probably request they chloroform me, so he could keep Oates. That kind of thinking wasn't much good.

There weren't many people around. A couple of jeeps drove up and some officers got out. There were some guys from a crash truck, and some stray Joes from the hangar gang.

Nobody said much.

You could feel the restlessness, and the unspoken wish that they'd hurry home and cut out this stalling.

In the old days when the Luftwaffe used to knock out whole squadrons, and half the ships landed at other bases, those sweat sessions used to be rough. Crew chiefs would be there, to see who made it.

At 2200 I decided our crew had probably had it.

Without me, their luck was bound to be bad. At 2205 I had laughed myself out of that and decided, without me their chances were about twenty percent better.

"I hope they all come back," somebody said simply.

The air was beginning to tighten and the wind seemed to pick up a little and grow cold. The sun was gone and night was just over the hill.

"I don't like this waiting." It was a girl's voice. "I wish they'd come."

It was one of the Red Cross girls from the Air Club. Maybe some gunner was her true love, maybe she was just down there for the hell of it. Anyway she wasn't enjoying it.

The minutes ticked off.

"God, why don't they come?" Some G.I.

The motors came faint out of the east, and grew into a heavy roar. The first group came over the field, and the low squadron peeled off. They were flying a beautiful tight formation. I guess they thought the Generals were still around.

The high group was just as pretty.

The Red Cross girl was counting out loud. They were home. They looked beautiful.

"Everybody made it," she announced. "Everybody."

I didn't wait around. It takes a long time to get everyone loaded, all the chutes and people in the truck, all the guns out of the turrets, all the bitches about the airplane written up on Form 1.

They were home. They didn't need me. I wasn't on that crew any more. I was way outside in the cool air.

I didn't know how I felt about it.

Sammy Newton's Crew

I didn't fly for a while. I was just a black dog around the squadron, an extra co-pilot.

Sam's crew was beginning to change. Bird was working at Group. Beach went away to the Flak House for a week.

Air crews are a lot like people. They have to grow up some time. Before Sam took his boys to Berlin the third time nobody thought much of the crew, except maybe the guys on the crew, and I never heard any of them making any great claims.

There were just six enlisted men assigned to an airplane. They got along all right, because there was a war on and you have to get along with the guys you fly with.

The Luftwaffe had taken itself deep into the homeland for a while, and taken to an extremely coy attitude. A couple of crews had whipped through thirty missions without even speaking to a 109 or a 190, by getting in on all the no-ball rides to France. The days of the Abbeville Kids and the Bastards from Brunswick were forgotten back in time.

With no fighting, it doesn't matter much who stands by the guns and swings the turrets around, and looks out the windows. Pilots tend to forget they may need gunners some afternoon. Gunners tend not to give a damn, and tend not to be eager about keeping their guns clean, and their eyes sweeping the sky for the enemy.

The twenty-first was the first time the Forts had been to Berlin since the invasion. The enlisted men had to grow up or fold up that day.

It wasn't the old crew. I was in the sack. Grant was grounded with a running nose. Parsons went along in his place. Bird was working up at Group, and Spaugh was flying in the nose. Mac, the Public Relations officer, went along for the ride. But the enlisted men were the original six.

The ride up across the North Sea was more or less normal, I guess. They didn't go on oxygen until halfway across. The sea was restfully free of flak guns as always and they didn't have any trouble. Oates did a lot of flying . . . good flying.

When the formations turned in at the coast, the VHF set came through with tidings of bandits.

Somebody up ahead was catching hell.

They were flying in the low squadron. A half hour before they reached Berlin, the low leader began to get feelings of insecurity and tucked up pretty tight. The wings were jammed in close together, and Sam was caught in a three-way squeeze, from the sides and on top and down under. And there was prop wash.

After almost chewing off the element leader's trailing edges, and almost having his own chewed off, Sam decided to get the hell up to an open shot in the high squadron.

He finessed out of the squeeze play and started pulling up. On the way somebody called a large formation of planes heading the wrong way.

At briefing there had been a lot of talk about the RAF tagging along behind on this ride, and really cooling this town for all time.

"Look at those damn Mosquitoes," Sam remembered saying.

"Those lucky bastards are on the way home," somebody else chimed in.

"Formation at nine o'clock level," Sharpe said.

Crone called them when they got around to seven. They were silver and they looked peaceable and went about their business in an orderly manner.

About that time Crone woke up. They weren't Mosquitoes. "Them are Me 410's," he announced.

They were turning in. Sharpe lined up on the lead ship. "Here they come." His voice wasn't much, he said later.

They were 410's all right, new ones with no paint. They came in on a tail-pass, just as Sam was slipping back into formation.

Sharpe squeezed down on the first one, and the first one squeezed down on Sharpe, and they kept on shooting at each other and kept on waiting.

Then Sharpe forgot to shoot any more and yelled, "I got one . . . I got one . . . I got one of those sonsabitches."

The Me sagged off and began to come apart. The top hatch spilled off and the pilot bailed out.

There were more.

The 20-millimeters were bursting all around the formation. Up ahead Forts were beginning to falter. One nosed out of formation in the group on the left and began to give birth. Nine chutes.

One old painted job out there at three o'clock had a fire in his Tokyos. Another tipped off on a wing and split-S-ed out of formation.

They queued up and came through again. Both sides were throwing everything. Sharpe's left feed went out, and he kept on shooting with one gun.

"Every time the ball opened up I thought we had it," Crone said later. "I could feel my ass being chewed off."

The ammunition covers fell off the ball, and Beach

Me 410

couldn't shoot straight down without losing all his ammunition.

Ross knocked off a 410 when the simple guy tried to pull in and fly formation while he lobbed shells into the group ahead.

"I could've conked the pilot with my gun barrel," Ross said. "But I decided to shoot him."

The 410 blew up.

Lewis tracked another across the tail, saw the pieces begin to chip off, and smoke belch out of the cowl, and the pilot came out streaming silk.

"Five o'clock high," somebody called.

"Coming in at nine," Mac said in the nose. It was a 190 going under to knock off a crippled Fort. Crone lined up on him straight-away low. It tipped over into a spin, spilling flame, and spun on into the ground.

"I watched him all the way," Crone said. "I just stood there and watched him with one eye, and waited for that other bastard with the other."

That other bastard came in from two o'clock high on the nose. Mac tagged him fair, saw him break up. Lewis called a bailed-out pilot and a falling wing.

The business was all back by the tail. Spaugh kept his guns swinging and did a lot of shooting, but they were all long-prayer shots, and he didn't claim anything more than a couple of scare-offs.

Oates and Sam were going nuts. Oates had to listen to VHF so he'd know what the leaders were doing. Sam was pleading with someone to tell him what was going on.

All the guns were shooting, and there were Forts and fighters throwing up all over the sky, and 20-millimeters splashing around.

"Where are they?" Sam said. "Anybody hit? Tail gunner? Waist gunner . . . where are they . . . radioman? What the hell's going on back there?"

"Sir," Sharpe said, in almost a scream, "will you please shut up?"

Sam decided the situation was under control.

The 410's made two main passes and several feints, and the side lines were thick with 109's and 190's looking for easy meat, waiting for wounded Forts to fall back.

Little Friends came on the scene then, 38's over the top and 51's in from high ten o'clock.

Sharpe was soaked with sweat. Crone wiped his forehead and came away with a cupful.

After two trips to Hamburg the flak was minor-league stuff, but it was rough, and it was everywhere . . . nothing but the little black puffs, though none of them were tracking along behind, or poking up to powder the nose.

Somebody up ahead said there were more bandits

in the area, but the Luftwaffe was through with Sam's crew.

"Check in," Sharpe said. "Everybody here? One okay. Two okay?"

Everybody checked in on time.

"We got one little hole in the right stabilizer," Crone said. "It ain't much."

"Godamighty, how'd we do it?" Sharpe asked. His hands were shaky and the sweat was draining down his back and puddling up in his electric shoes. He turned the electricity off, and he still sweated.

Sam crawled back through the bomb bays on an inspection tour. Crone was stroking his gun kindly. Beach was moaning about his gun covers. Sharpe was still sweating.

"Hey, Crone," Sharpe called up. "I guess you checked out that shooting iron today."

Nobody hurt. No holes to speak of.

Sam didn't really believe it. Probably a wing would fall off before long.

"Got a roochie?" he asked Ross.

Ross had a pack of sweat-soaked Luckies, and everybody in the waist had one. Everybody had two.

Lewis even took time out in the top turret and had one.

The let-down was restful. The formations had loosened up out in the Channel. At 12,000 Oates told everybody to take off their oxygen masks and relax.

England came through on time on course.

"On flight plan," Parsons said. First word of the day.

I met them at interrogation. They looked like they hadn't slept for a year. All of them got pretty jagged on the scotch. They were all talking with both hands and drinking coffee and dunking doughnuts and trying to get more scotch.

John Nilson, a fraternity brother of Sam and me, was doing the interrogating, and he couldn't hear any answers to his questions, because every time he got someone steadied down to coherent accounting, somebody like me from the outside would come in and paw the boys over and ask if it was really true, five of those bastards.

"Probably six," said Sharpe. "Lewis is only claiming one, but he got two."

"Maybe," Lewis said.

"You might as well claim," Sharpe said. "We won't get 'em anyway."

Finally S2 cleared the interrogating room and everybody had to stand at the door and watch Sam beam on his club.

Every ten seconds somebody else would say, "Brother, I thought we'd had it."

Or, "I was halfway out that hatch."

Or, "Did you see those poor bastards on fire?"

Or, "You should've seen us."

Madhouse.

Sharpe came out of the briefing hut with most of his clothes off, talking to Crone who was talking right back at him. Two guys from Black's crew came up and grabbed them.

"Sure was a sweet goddamn job of shooting," they said.

Sharpe laughed. "You ought to see my left gun barrel."

"Like a goddamn corkscrew," Crone said.

"First time I ever knew you could pray and cuss in the same sentence," Sharpe said. I think he read that, but it must have been true, because he said it three or four times.

Oates went away with the sack of kits. He was shot, and the scotch had almost knocked him off. Parsons went with him. He had to turn in his log.

Sam came into the equipment room wearing his two .45's.

"Some outfit you got, Sambo," somebody said.

"A hot bunch of operators," somebody else said.

"Don't tell me your troubles," Sam said. "The chaplain's right outside. I've told you a thousand times I got the best crew."

He hadn't told anyone. He hadn't even thought so himself. But he thought so then.

The sky showed blue out the window. The flagpole showed red, white, and blue.

A DOLL NAMED AUGUST

August wrote to Sam and asked him when my birthday was. Sam wanted to see what she'd send, so he told her some number in June and then forgot about it.

She sent me a big hunk of soap shaped like a canteen, with a cord on it to hang around my neck.

"Ain't it romantic?" Sam said.

"Ain't it?"

It was nice soap.

Then she sent me some canned deviled ham and some powdered noodle soup, about ten packages, and some cheese that smelled ghastly.

There is still some soup left.

She was still sending me poems. Maybe she was making them up, maybe plagiarizing.

The last was:

"My one romance is far off in the past
It ended with the time I saw you last
I've met so many others since that night

But none like you could thrill me with delight.
I had a new sensation with you in my arms
And now when I recall your laughing eyes, your
    charms
I understand the reason for my frets
You're still my only love, my one romance."

Then she wrote, "Please bear with me in my contemporary moments or something and please don't be embarrassed. Write soon."

I can't prove it, but I think that one is copyrighted.

15

FINIS

They kept on flying and I kept on sitting on the ground. The crew finished up on a Leipzig haul, mostly.

Beach still had four to do. Ross finished up the day before. Bird and I had an even dozen.

The final gesture used to be a buzz job. Come home and show the people how glad you are it's over.

But Sam didn't care if anyone knew or not. He just flew that airplane home and put it on the ground the quickest way possible. I ran alongside and waved all the way in. I felt sort of drunk. They were all through.

Sam had a huge grin on his face.

Nobody was crazy happy. They all seemed to be in a quiet daze. I mauled everyone a little, and figured they'd feel like mauling back, but they just grinned and went on unloading guns and flak suits.

Everyone is supposed to get thrown in the drink after his last one. There wasn't any water.

Sam was telling Roy about number one supercharger.

Grant had finished them up too. He was smiling all over and bitching about no buzz job.

"Lieutenant Benson, I presume," I said.

"Old bertstiles," he said.

"You're all through."

"We're all through." He was like the others, a little coked-up and sunstruck.

And then I saw they wouldn't believe it for hours, maybe days. It would come slow. They knew it now, but they'd believe it later. They'd begin to believe it when Porada came through and woke up the guy in the next bed and didn't say a word to any of them. They'd begin to believe it when they lay in the sack and listened to the engines kick over, and the planes take off.

Bird and I went into the equipment room ahead and filled up a half dozen flak helmets with water.

"I christen thee a sharp son of a bitch," I said to Sharpe. He tried to retreat, but I nailed him cold.

Lewis was drinking some coffee and I poured a bucketful around his ears.

"You're a hard man," he said.

Bird got Sam in the hall and stopped to think how sweet it was going to be, and Sam knocked the flak helmet out of his hands, and Bird got the whole thing down the front of him.

Crone was in hiding. Grant holed up behind a locker. Crone came out after a while and I drowned him.

Authority showed up right after.

"Was that you?" he said. First Lieutenant Equipment Officer.

"That was me," I said. "That was I."

"Get a mop."

"Later."

Bird and I got Benson. Later I got a mop.

It kept going through me. They were all through, and I had twelve to do. They were going home, and I was staying here. They were the crew I came with, and they were leaving me behind.

Lonely One

Sometimes London is the loneliest city in the world, and the loneliness hangs over the city like a curse. And out of all the millions of Englishmen and Scots and Americans and Poles and Frenchmen and Czechs and all the others, there is no one.

I had dinner at the Savoy and drank a whole bottle of wine, and that on top of the scotch I drank all afternoon tightened up the loneliness and deepened the lostness.

The buzz bombs were coming over steadily, and a sort of hellish pressure seemed to be on everyone. Hour after hour, night after night, day after day, since just after D-day they had been coming, with no letup and no end in sight.

The world was pretty shaky. I needed someone to look at across the table, someone to talk to for a while . . . just someone, anyone . . . but I was alone.

In the end I went down in the underground and took the tube to Piccadilly. From Piccadilly I went to King's Cross, and then back to Waterloo, then Leicester Square again, then somewhere else to somewhere else. There were people anyway.

I spoke to several. There was a Canadian who got off at Waterloo bound for somewhere south, and a South African Red Cross girl, who had to be back for a date in Cambridge two hours ago, and there was a dubious blonde who thought I was trying to pick her up, and maybe I was.

Finally I got tired of riding the trains and got off at Bond Street station. I stood there, wondering where to go, and what good it would do. It would be just the same anywhere.

I almost stepped on a little girl. It was so close I involuntarily knelt down to see if she was hurt. She was asleep.

Then I looked around. The cave dwellers were getting their cave ready for the night. The bunks were all taken and most of the floor space was covered with blankets and coats and papers, families bedding down. An old man with a beard was reading a paper-bound book in the harsh light by some steps to somewhere.

The little girl had white-gold hair all thrown around, and her lips were parted a little. Her mother, I guess it was her mother, lay on a blanket on the cement with another child, maybe a boy, maybe not.

I checked the double-decker bunks along the wall. They were all full. A weary-faced woman was looking at me. I tried to smile, but it didn't come off very well. She didn't smile back. Maybe she was out of smiles by this tail end of the day.

It was hot, and the smell of all the people pressed in from everywhere and sucked around the corners when the trains passed.

A man and his wife and two little kids were trying to get set over in a corner. One of the little kids was crying. The man had his shirt off, and his underwear was several days old. He had a tired face, but there was gentleness in his eyes, and his voice was steady when he quieted the child.

I looked back at the little girl, still kneeling, and she was looking at me.

She didn't seem to be scared. I'd never seen eyes so blue before . . . not blue like the sky, but warmer, softer, and sort of bewildered and strangely sweet.

"Hello," I said, "I thought I stepped on you." I wanted her to know how it was.

She didn't say anything, just kept looking at me. I figured she was about three, maybe three and a quarter.

"How old are you?"

"Five." Her voice was sleepy.

She sure didn't look five.

"Want some gum?" It was the only thing I could think of.

She shook her head.

"I do." It was a boy I hadn't seen before, in shorts, with the dirtiest knees in London. But his face was clean, and his hand was pretty much so.

I gave him the whole package. It was Beechnut.

"Thanks, Yank." His voice was shrill and high, and then he disappeared.

"You better go back to sleep." I said to the little girl.

"I can't."

Her mother was awake now. I smiled to reassure her.

"I have to go somewhere," the little girl said sadly.

I thought that over a minute.

"I'll take her," I said to her mother.

Her eyes were blue too, and they softened when she looked at me.

"Want to go with me?" to the little girl.

"Yes."

I lifted her up high for a good look. She didn't weigh anything at all, and then I put her on my shoulders and she gave a little delighted gasp, and we were off.

I took her up one side of the escalator, and down the other, and whirled her around in a couple of circles, but that was rougher on me than it was on her, so we stopped that, and rode the escalator again.

She was laughing all the time, but the only way I could tell was by the vibration on the back of my neck. I guess she didn't want to wake anyone.

The trains were roaring by every few seconds.

Two women, sitting with their backs to the wall, knitting, smiled up at me. A one-legged man, reading Proust, looked up from his seat. He wore thick glasses, and his lips didn't move, but someway there was friendliness in the look, before he went back to Proust.

The little girl tapped me on the ear. "Over there."

I steered her over in front of the sign and put her down.

"I won't be long," she said shyly.

The sharp odor of the antiseptic mixed with the odor of the people and the smoke and the food. A very fat woman was breaking a sausage in two over on one side.

The little girl was back. Her eyes were even bluer.

"Prettiest eyes in this town," I told her.

She laughed and her cheeks glowed, and we went off to ride the escalator again.

I had a bad time finding my way back to the right blanket and the right mother. We wandered all over that part of London, but finally the little girl navigated us home.

Everyone was looking at me, but I didn't care much.

The mother was asleep again, her breath made a soft little whistle, her arm thrown slackly over the other child in a gesture of complete exhaustion.

"Thank you very much." The little girl lay down again on the cement and covered herself up with a coat. Her eyes showed that deep blue for a moment and then she closed them.

I stood over her then and my mind moved back a couple of years. Somewhere back there, somewhere, a long time ago, there were beds and sheets and blankets, and moonlight and a fresh wind coming through the window into my room. And somewhere over there, across an ocean, a thousand years ago, there had been laughter and peace and love at times.

I looked around.

Peace was just a word here, just a wish to the new moon, just a prayer to every dawn. But for a little while there had been laughter, quiet laughter from a little girl who didn't want to wake anybody, while the trains screamed through the tunnels, deep below the war outside.

And there was love . . . all around . . . and suddenly it pressed in stronger than the fear or the deadly tiredness or the smell of so many people.

It wasn't until I was almost back at the Red Cross Club that I realized that the loneliness had gone.

16

NEW CREW

When I got back from London, I was on Green's crew.

I didn't know Green very well. He lived upstairs in the co-pilots' house. He moved in when some guy went to Switzerland. He was a checked-out co-pilot. He'd never had a crew before.

I saw him back at the house.

"I guess you're stuck with me," I said.

"You mean you're stuck with me."

We grinned at each other.

"I think you'll like the boys," he said quietly.

I liked the way he talked. He told me a little about each of them. We'd talked a little one night, so I knew something about him. He'd lived in the Philippines. He'd gone to some queer kind of progressive school or college called Deep Valley, and switched to Stanford just before the war for Pre-Med.

"Some day, I'll go back to it," he said.

So neither of us were in it for life, we hoped. The sooner we got it over with, the better.

Then he said, "I'm glad it was you."

There wasn't much I could say. He had me closed in. Nobody had ever been glad that I was on their club before. But I think he meant it. Anyway, I wasn't some new joker on his first mission. I had twenty in my background.

"Okay," I said. "Maybe we'll stay lucky."

We shook hands on it, because it was the only thing we could think of.

I'd been dreading going back, but it was all right after that. Anything he ever said to me was all right. He just had a way of saying things.

"Okay," I said. "Take it easy."

After that I went down to Public Relations to check on the files of the crew.

John W. Green was listed as a Second Lieutenant from a place called Tujunga, California.

The original navigator, Johnny O'Leary, was so good he was flying only lead ships.

The new navigator, Martin L. Bulion, came from the big town and was a student at NYU before the war. He was a flight officer.

I already knew First Lieutenant Simmers a little. He was the bombardier (Robert L. the records said). He has a wife in Detroit.

The top-turret man had been a bottle inspector in the Old Reading Brewery, a guy named Bradley (Gilbert) from Shamokin, Pennsylvania, a Technical Sergeant. A combination of Shamokin and the Old Reading Brewery sounded pretty rugged to me.

Technical Sergeant Thomas F. McAvoy was listed as

the radioman. He came from Lawrence, Massachusetts, and he'd been a railway traffic man in better days.

Green had said Bossert, the ball-turret gunner, was a quiet classic of a gunner. He was a Staff Sergeant named Harlyn L., and he'd worked in one of Hamilton Beach's factories, and lived in Cassville, Wisconsin.

The waist-gunner, Tolbert (Roy H.), was supposed to be the crew clown. He'd been a mechanic and a clerk in a cotton mill down in Greenwood, South Carolina.

Staff Sergeant Ervin E. Mock was the tail-gunner, and in the mood to check out as an engineer. He'd worked at Douglas and he came from Hobart, Oklahoma, and Green said he was the best tail-gunner in the business.

I couldn't tell much from the papers. The reason I checked at all, I wanted to know their names before I flew a mission with them. But by the time I got out the door I'd forgotten which name went with which position.

Mock . . . tail . . . Bradley . . . waist . . . no, ball . . . no, Tolbert is the ballman . . . no . . .

In the end I was only sure Green would sit on the left side, and I'd sit on the right, and maybe it would come out all right.

Education

Our first one was to Munich.

I didn't even get to bed. I was brushing my teeth when Porada came through with the usual announcement.

The round trip there and back takes ten hours.

There was a ten-tenths overcast, which meant we didn't see the wine country or the Rhine or the snow on the Jungfrau, or anything at all of the world except the sky, and the sun on the cloud cover.

Most of the Forts got home. A few blew up. A few Libs sank down through the undercast to be knocked off by the Focke-Wulfs at their leisure.

The only way I could tell it was Munich was by the flak. For ten hours we were cut off from the world by the soup.

"You think we hit Munich," Mock called up on the way home.

"Damn right," Simmers said. "Where do you think that flak came from, Coney Island?"

Nobody laughed.

"Sort of wonderful," Mock said thoughtfully. "Sort of horrible, I mean."

"We got some smart sonsabitches on our side," Tolbert came in in his slow drawl. "Them jokers know everything."

When the forever of the trip back to England was over, and the ship was checked away for the night, Green and I sat there for a minute and thought it over. Not so bad. Long day, but not so bad. We'd worked all right together. He grinned at me.

I lay on the floor of the truck going in, and almost went to sleep before we got to the equipment hut.

There was a stray bomb-aimer at interrogation who said he knew a place up on the Cambridge road where they sold strawberries.

"Come on," he said. "Fresh strawberries. Big red ones."

"I'm coming."

Fresh strawberries were sort of impossible, a dream like milkshakes and Sun Valley and riding the waves on the beach below La Jolla.

We found the place where the strawberries grew, and

B-24 Liberator

found the guy who sold them, and tried to buy him out. He would only sell us four pounds each.

On the way back we passed a school. There were some kids playing Spitfires and Messerschmitts in the school yard.

"Maybe we ought to give them some?" Pete said.

We stopped and yelled to the kids. "Hey, want some strawberries?"

Four of them came running, three boys and a girl, and one little girl stayed behind and hid behind a tree. They had dirty knees and dirty hands, and they were all more or less blondes.

The first boy took a very small green strawberry.

"Take a big one," I said. "Take a handful."

"Take it easy," Pete said. "You got all day."

They were shy about it, but they each dug out a good-sized handful, snickering to themselves and looking down at the ground.

"Take a handful for the little dame behind the tree," Pete said.

So they did, and then ran away over to the school steps and sat there giggling and stuffing the strawberries into their mouths.

I took another good look at the school before we pushed off again. With all the rest of England so green, the school yard was dusty and as bare as concrete. With all the rest of England around there so soft and quietly lovely, that school and school yard had a hard ugliness that stayed in my mind.

Half a mile down the road we came to a great lane of trees that led up to a big old castle of a country house, a good mile away.

"Let's stop and eat these things," Pete said.

We left the bikes outside the fence and went through the gate, because it was unlocked, and found a good tree to flop down under.

The sun filtered through the leaves, and the grass had a cool, sweet smell to it, and for a minute I felt a sense of peace, a quiet wave of relief came over me.

But when I listened I could hear planes. Without looking I knew they were fighters, coming home from shooting up the roads to Paris probably. Then a bunch of Halifaxes came over high, towing gliders, and Pete and I watched them go off toward Cherbourg.

"Remember when you went to school?" Pete asked.

I nodded. I remembered that far back. Apparently we both had that school in our minds.

It was just like a thousand schools in America, sort of stuck in somewhere, like it didn't really belong at all, small and battered and overworked-looking.

I didn't go to a school like that. . . . The English equivalent of an American grade school . . . for little kids.

I went through the Denver Public School system, and pretty red-hot schools they were supposed to be too.

Politics didn't bother those Denver schools particularly. The teachers always got paid on time, and the buildings were fairly adequate. Some of the old sections of town had old beat-up schools, but when a new section grew up the people usually got a new grade school to go with it.

I went to Washington Park School. I started out there in kindergarten and went all the way up through the sixth grade. I learned to read and write and add and subtract and do long division.

I could remember Miss Wood in the first grade. She shook hell out of me in the hall one day, just on general principles, and told my mother I was probably mentally defective.

My mother saw to it I got on the ball with a cadence-count after that.

And there was Miss Chrysinger, who racked me back in the third grade for laughing at a little girl when her dress flew up and showed her drawers. She made me apologize to the girl after school.

And there was Miss Myers, who was a fiend on birdhouses, and had everyone in her class building birdhouses, and Miss Lickty (or something like that), who used to come in when we were sliding on our stomachs in the shower room, and stand there, and after a while tell us to cut it out, you're making too much noise.

There was Mrs. Pacal, who kept me out in the hall all one afternoon giving me hell for calling some joker a liar. She said I didn't deserve to be in the Cub Scouts, and I was a disgrace to the neckerchief, and anybody that used the word liar was likely to go straight to hell, soon.

We used to start every morning in sixth grade the same way. Mrs. Pacal had the whole class stand and recite a poem, beginning with "vigor, virility, vim and pep . . ." and going on with more of the same, only more so.

It was strange the way I felt about Washington Park School. Looking back, I approved of almost everything that went on there. It was probably the best school I ever went to.

They taught their kids to read and write, to honor their fathers and mothers, to salute the flag, and brush their teeth. They vaccinated everybody, and the scrawny ones got milk and graham crackers at ten in the morning, and there was a play festival in the spring where all the schools danced, and we always sang carols at Christmas time.

They did their best, all the way around, at Washington Park School. After fire drills, when everyone was safely out in the sun, we never went back in again without pledging allegiance to the flag and to the country for which it stands . . . one nation indivisible . . . with liberty and justice for all.

Maybe they were just words then, but there was a quiet sort of majestic feeling that went with them, like we were part of something big and good that would last forever.

Washington Park started getting me ready for this, I thought, for B-17's in England, and strawberries in the grass, and Munich through the overcast, and Berlin with the 190's slow-rolling through the formation, and the flak of Paris, and the flak of Posen, and the flak of Kiel.

"I sure had fun in school," Pete said.

"Yeah," I agreed mechanically. It was fun all right.

After Washington Park I went to junior high school, two miles away, down across the park, for seventh, eighth, and ninth grades.

That was a bad time in a lot of ways. There was

always something about sex to worry about, and to try and look up in dictionaries. The girls all started to get cagey and fill out, and the boys mostly had pimples, and I had to learn how to dance.

I couldn't remember many of the teachers. Mrs. Fowler taught English and Latin in the ninth. She was wonderful because she liked kids and she loved books, and someway she could give that love away.

I could remember a new course about the American Dream, by a little sparrow of a social science teacher who looked like she'd never dreamed any kind of dream in her life.

Miss Thomson taught algebra with character-building on the side. She died right after I left.

"Remember high school," Pete laughed a sad sort of a laugh. "Boy, we really shook things around in high school."

I took another strawberry and remembered high school, South High School.

The building faced west, and the tower had a clock with four faces that never agreed, because the pigeons used to sit on the hands. There were 2500 kids and the football team wore purple satin pants, and we won the city championship in '36 and '37, and I sat on the bench and yelled and watched.

I was involved in an outfit called the Progressive Education Group, with forty picked members from the two feeding junior high schools, picked for character and brains and general affability. We stayed together all the way through high school. We were a hot outfit all right . . . two teachers and forty eager beavers on our way to the moon.

The School Board signed away all its powers. We could take a shot at anything, any subject, any whim, for as long or as short as we desired. We could pick our courses and our teachers. We could go on field trips, and use the school bus. We could do anything we chose, for two hours of the school day.

The first year it was three hours a day. Progressive English one hour a day, progressive social science one hour (the names didn't mean anything), and progressive science one hour.

Progressive science turned out to be a spectacular flop and was discontinued. Each member of the class chose some scientific subject to investigate and report on to the others. It took a year to give all the reports.

I chose sleeping bags, and the science of keeping warm in one, and made a gala report on this in April, and just sat there and slept the rest of the year.

I think my report had something to do with their discontinuing the course.

Mr. Arnold and Miss Aronson were the faculty members assigned to the class for the three-year ride. Streamlined educators, interested in the latest trending of the adolescent mind.

I could remember most of the educational byways that class flung itself down . . . a speed-up course in psychology (Mr. Arnold's particular field), a quick survey of adolescent sex problems. We started to produce a series of plays and never finished. I was supposed to neck Jane, a girl in one of them, but it folded before we got around to rehearsing that scene.

We wrote poems and short stories, and seriously delved into the art of letter writing. We spent one spring learning the stories of operas. We debated whether to spend a little time on history, and decided not.

We spoke extemporaneously. We spoke out of turn. We ranted and raised hell and went out on field trips and took in the key movies, and had a few parties to develop social poise.

We took turns sitting in front of the class, listening to a frank personality dissection, asking for it, eager for the good of the soul . . . a purely objective critique.

Mostly we made reports on how we were doing, how we were coming along in our growth, evaluating the expansion of our personalities, the bloom of our egos.

The whole experiment crowned off with a final six weeks of our senior year of going out in the world, and holding down a job all afternoon, without pay, to see how the world really is. One guy went to an architect's office, one to a bank, one to a hospital, the girls scattered around to schools and social-work clinics and around.

I chose the Forest Service and spent six weeks looking over fish-stocking reports, finding out where the best fishing was. I left every day just before 1500 hours to get back to baseball practice.

When we made our reports at the end, I stated I hadn't gotten a whole hell of a lot out of it. That was when my relationship with Mr. Arnold became undone. There was a time when I felt deep admiration for his smooth ways.

He was going to show the report to Mr. Corey (Principal) and wash me out as a total progressive failure. So I went in and hooked the report off his desk, threw it away, and sat up all night writing a new one, and went on the record as having learned a lot about the Forest Service, deeply appreciating the wonderful chance for inside study, and agreeing it was a fine worth-while way to spend my last year in high school.

It was either sell myself out or come back to South High for another year, so I sold myself out. Afterward I was going to go back and kick hell out of Mr. Arnold. Unfinished business.

"I sure had a big time in high school," Pete said yearningly. "Wish I was back there now."

But I didn't. The best day of my life was when I got out of high school.

Maybe that was where my education really went bad. I started to slack off right after I got there.

After a year of plane geometry I stopped taking math. I decided I wouldn't need any more, since I wasn't going to be an engineer or a math prof.

I didn't need any mental discipline.

I could remember Miss Morrison, a tiny white-haired woman, who made us memorize every theorem, word for word, and every step of the proof, step by step in order, just for the good of the mind. She took every other Friday off to make a speech and try to set us straight on a few things.

She was the first person I remember who thought the world was going to hell, because the people in it are lazy and undisciplined thinkers and getting soft. She said math is good for you, because it makes you think coherently and logically and reasonably, and all the way through to a solution.

I took physics too, and didn't get along with the teacher, and almost flunked out when I wrote up an experiment on Wheatstone's Bridge, and concluded it was a total waste of time.

I could see no value in understanding the principles of the universe.

I took chemistry in senior grade, from Mr. Bush, the same teacher who taught us progressive science when I was a sophomore. Mr. Bush was a nice guy and still progressive. He divided his class into two groups, the ones who thought they might be able to use chemistry later, or at least a little background of lab technique, and those who just wanted a general knowledge.

I took the General Background Course, because I was getting lazier and lazier. And now I can't even tell what a valence is. I didn't learn how to handle the simplest lab equipment.

In an age where the chemists are shaking the world down to its components, and synthesizing a whole new world of incredible potentialities, I can't even remember what a benzine ring looks like, and wouldn't know how to start a quantitative analysis, and hardly know the difference between a compound and a mixture.

"Air is a mixture," I said out loud.

"What?" Pete sat up.

"Nothing," I said.

Air is now, I thought, all the time. Air was what I'd ended up in, the air over Brunswick and Hamburg and Stettin.

The progressives hold that a kid knows what he wants, he can be trusted to choose wisely, and knows where he wants to go, and will work like a peasant to get there. He knows what will make him a strong citizen, and a wised-up member of the world community.

Maybe some kids do.

We held a mock election on the fourteenth of November, 1936. Landon won something like 26 to 14.

I remembered the way the class jumped on our newswriting teacher when she said the sit-down-strikers might have something on their side.

South High was full of nice kids. There were three or four Negroes, and a few Dutch kids from a colony out near the brickyards, and a Chinese or two, and not any Japs that I remember, and not any Italians . . . just Americans, mostly solid middle-income-bracket Americans.

We never studied about war. We never hunted around for the causes of wars, or talked about prevention of future wars. I didn't think there would be any more wars. People would never get roped in again, the world couldn't be that dumb again.

There were courses in homemaking and sewing and cooking and shop and business and typing, but the Progressive Education Group didn't mess with them much.

I did learn to type.

There was a course in economics, but not many people took it. It wasn't required of anyone.

There was unlimited talk about the integration of the personality, and living a rounded life, and developing the subtler facts of character. There wasn't any mention of blood and guts and sweat, and get in there and dig, dig, dig, except in football practice.

There was a war in Spain then, and a war in China.

There were people then who were saying that all wars are for all the people, and sooner or later, inevitably all the people will become involved, because that is the way the war is now, unless something is done to remove the causes.

But nothing was done.

"I'm gonna go to college after this," Pete said. "If the Government is willing to pay for it, I'm gonna go. Everybody ought to go to college."

"Sure," I said.

That's what my folks thought. I guess they planned on it before I was born. And they saved enough to see me through when the time came.

I went to Colorado College at the foot of Pikes Peak.

I signed up for economic history and biology and medieval and modern history and English, my freshman year.

I had enough money for tuition and books, enough for a fraternity, with a tight squeeze. The fraternity got me a board job washing dishes, and I worked an NYA job, minding the ski tow on Sundays, to round out my finances.

My English prof was a guy named Powell with a beard and a mind. He could take out on music or Shakespeare or baseball or Schopenhauer, wrestling or Milton, drinking and Ring Lardner, Browning and women. He had known Thomas Wolfe and he was supposed to be writing a fourteen-year-old book on Byron.

Powell opened doors I'd never known were there before, and gave me a desire to learn that I never had before, to start then before it was too late, to know something about the world before I was too deep in it to care any more.

And then Powell said the hell with it and took off for seclusion. There was a rumor the college wouldn't raise his salary. Maybe he planned to finish the book on Byron, or just contemplate the universe. After he left, it was never the same.

I stayed there off and on for three years, knocking around trying to find another Powell, learning to drink, falling in love a couple of times a year, roaming around in the summers looking for an easy life, trying to figure out a way into the clear.

The college newspaper came through with a front-page editorial in the spring of '41, a poster-type thing, with a face staring out through the words, "TRAVEL, ADVENTURE, EDUCATION . . . join the Army and get your gonads shot off. . . ."—something on that order.

It was that kind of a school, remote from the world where the storm troopers quietly rode into Paris, detached from the world where the English kids drank their tea and took the Spitfires up for the late afternoon flight, oblivious of the world where Chinese were raped and starved and slaughtered.

The faculty was split up over the war. Some of them faced it, some of them turned away. Some of them said we would be in it soon, should be in it now . . . some said no. . . .

Everyone had heard of Nanking and what happened there, everyone read about Poland. Everyone had read about atrocity stories in the last war, too. Some people, though, admitted these new atrocity stories were probably true, and then shrugged and had another double bourbon.

"I don't know whether I'll go back or not," I said.

A good library and the chance to talk to a few men of wisdom might be a surer way.

I have to know some more about economics. I have to read a lot more history and sociology and philosophy. I can get all that in a library, if I could just talk it over afterward with a person or persons who know something about it.

If I could talk to people like Doctor Beard, and Stuart Chase, and Erwin Edman . . . might as well shoot the moon . . . might as well say Shakespeare and Tolstoy and Jesus Christ. . . .

I rolled over and lay on my back looking at the sky.

A Mosquito came over, revving up about 3000, headed for the Reich, on a nuisance raid to Berlin maybe, a 4000-pounder to keep the people on their toes . . . or on their knees. . . .

"I got to learn something," Pete said. "I don't know anything except how to look through a bombsight and toggle out the bombs."

179

Mosquito

The Army has a big stake in education, but Congress put the knife in the college end of it.

I remembered my Army education. The flying part was all right. It got the planes in the air, and the bombs to Berlin. But there were weeks of eight classes a day in Preflight, and ground school all the way through, and the Aviation Cadet attempt at education was the saddest, poorest, most incomplete I ever ran into.

The Air Force started out with the admirable idea that a flier should know something about the principles of flight, and something of the sciences and arts which have made flight possible. Then a minimum time was set up to transplant all this into an airman's mind while at the same time teaching him to march, and make up his sack, and fly a plane, and it just didn't work out.

They gave it to you in big simple doses, and told you the answers if you didn't catch on, because they needed fliers, and couldn't wash out more than a set percentage.

The Army has the right idea about making education possible for everyone, no matter who or where from, but the Army way of putting it across, giving the maximum of

180

predisgested information in the minimum time, with no time to think it over, or talk it over, is a pretty bad way of doing things, and only justified in an emergency.

"We're doing all right on these strawberries," Pete said. "You're almost four pounds heavier."

"Just about fed up," I said.

I wasn't thinking so much of strawberries. There was something sickeningly wrong with all that education when I looked back on it. Most of it was my fault.

But maybe the worst thing of all, most people would think it was a good education, the people who paid for most of it, those who haven't had a chance to get in that much school time themselves.

Maybe it could have been a good education, if I had done some work on it. Certainly it could have been a hell of a lot better.

But there is something wrong with the whole system, from the way it was set up to the way it is finally dished out.

I picked out another strawberry, and lay back and tried to think it through.

A group of Liberators was going out. Calais, probably, to try and knock out the flying-bomb installations.

The flying bombs were a pretty good example of what advanced education could bring.

How about the little school down the road? Dirty little schoolhouse, but no dirtier and no more inadequate than thousands of others in Canada and Nebraska and Bavaria and West Virginia, and a whole lot better than most schools in North China and south Normandy and the middle islands of Japan, and a hell of a lot better than no school at all.

Schools should be the cleanest, prettiest, best-built, most carefully planned and put-together buildings of a society. There shouldn't be such a vast difference between a place like Yale or Ohio State or even South High and Slate Creek School up on the Blue River in Colorado. Schools should be built better and kept up better than banks, because there is a whole lot more wealth in them.

But the buildings don't matter as much as the teachers in them, the instructors and professors and coaches. Powell was the best teacher I ever had, and I guess Mrs. Fowler and Miss Morrison come next. Powell quit because it wasn't worth it. He couldn't live on the money he was getting. Miss Morrison has probably retired, and before the war there was always a lot of mad talk about kicking out married teachers. Maybe Mrs. Fowler has had it.

I'd read about all the hell raised in this country, when a Bill came up in Parliament to give women teachers equal pay.

Oh, God! what a world.

When a civilization pays professors $1800 a year, and pimps and jockeys and swoon-singers triple and fifty times the dough, then something is likely to go wrong in that civilization, sooner or later.

I read somewhere that education is the biggest business in America, bigger than garments or policy or steel, but the war is taking education for a hell of a ride, and those others seem to be doing fine.

Lost education is harder to catch up than shortages in .50-caliber armor piercing, or bombers or knitting needles. But a shortage of men with wisdom, to run the world, has always been the most acute shortage on the books, men with enough background to know what has been, and who have some idea of what may come next, and at least a wry dream of what might come next. . . .

"Where would you go if you were me?" Pete said.

"Depends on what you want to do," I said slowly. "Depends on a lot of things."

In the end it comes down to what should an education really do?

"Hutchins claims he can help you to learn to think, if you go to Chicago or St. Johns," I said out loud.

"Jesus," Pete laughed, "Talk sense, tell me something practical."

I laughed, too, but it was a lousy laugh.

If Hutchins could really teach people to think, he should run the whole educational setup.

A few barrels of thought, or a few carloads, liberally distributed among all the people, might open up the world for some sunny weather.

I thought of trying to go to St. Johns or Chicago for a while. If the war ever ends, and the luck still holds, I still might. But I don't know whether reading the great books and studying what the big wheels of the past have said and written will solve even my own problem.

An education should try to teach a man how to think all right, and failing in that, should at least teach him a little humility, and try to get him to open his mind, and keep him cagey about what he takes in, and keep him ever reminded that there are many people of all sorts of blood strains and color phases, all essentially pretty much like him. It should teach him that he is part of mankind.

I thought again about Mrs. Pacal in the sixth grade. Maybe it would have been better if the class had started every day with the words Hemingway took from John Donne, ". . . for I am a piece of mankind . . . any man's death diminishes me . . ." instead of "vigor, virility, vim and pep. . . ."

Some more Liberators came over. Probably the first

wings in were dropping their bombs now. People were dying. The bloody dirt of France was taking another beating.

An education should give a man the facts about his world . . . straight. It should tell the little American kids there aren't many bathrooms in Sinkiang, and not enough toothbrushes in Turkey, and not enough honest democratic government in Chicago or Jersey City or the District of Columbia, or any city in any district for that matter.

That education should include just as much information about the world as possible, how people live and where, and what they disagreed over in the past, and why they are going to have to get in close in the future, or there won't be any future.

An education should give a person some idea of how a society functions, through the dreams and laws and practices and theories of economics. The idea should be spread around that economics is just a hell of a name for the way people live together. People have to work, and the study of what they do, and how they do it and why, is the study of economics, and it includes just about everything done by mankind, to mankind, for mankind.

An education should include a pretty complete mathematical and scientific background, as illuminating and extensive as possible, the best that good teaching and imaginative text writing can dream up, plus a lot of movies, things like Disney's evolution sequence in *Fantasia*. The math shouldn't stop in the sixth grade or the eighth or the twelfth. It should go all the way through, because it keeps the brain clicking over. It is an antidote for lazy thinking. You either think in a math class or you wash out.

For the other side of it, the literature and the music and the arts and languages, they should give you a shot at the best there is, and not care too much if it doesn't work at first. They should find teachers who are in love with their stuff, people like Powell and Mrs. Fowler, teachers who can see some of the magic inside, and open the door for those who cannot see very well at first.

When the great books and the best plays and the loveliest music are considered dull by most of the people of a generation it is the fault of unsympathetic teaching and unimaginative presentation and not enough teaching or presentation.

Two P-47's came skipping over the hedges, going north for home. They still had their belly tanks.

"I don't want to be a dumb bastard all my life," Pete said. "I want to know something some day."

P-47 Thunderbolt

Most everyone wants to know something at some time in his life, probably. The desire to learn, the desire to see and find out is deep in a great many people, but it gets knocked out early in most, or wrapped up in the white paper of a diploma, or a little more securely in the sheepskin of a degree.

Intellectual curiosity is more or less dormant in most people, but a good teacher can give it a shot in the arm, just by being a good teacher, and giving the curious one something to work with.

Education is a lifetime affair, and should be, and could be, and must be a whole lot more so. With the war taking everyone out of the schools early in America and England, and with the schools practically closed down in occupied Europe and sold out and emasculated in Germany, and just about the same in China and India and the Islands, a whole generation is forked by the numbers.

"The trouble is," Pete said, "even when you do learn something it's liable to screw you up."

"I guess you're right," I said.

Bombardiering is probably like that, and the simple art of throwing the knee into some guy's testicles before he slits your throat.

Maybe all education has to be built around two words . . . Truth . . . and Justice . . . and maybe if it was, after a long slow time some sort of a halfway decent world could be worked out.

Maybe there ought to be some more phrases like "take it easy" and "step back and laugh at it sometimes" to build around to, so the somber bright-eyed ones don't throw in the blue laws or come up with something like National Socialism.

"Have another strawberry," Pete said. "You look like you've seen the light. What the hell's wrong with you?"

I laughed and sat up and looked at the sun.

If there was only some way to have the most re-spected men in the world stand up once a month and tell all the people that they are just people, and there is such a hell of a lot to do and learn, that thinking you are wise is just about the quickest way to prevent anything good being done and the easiest way of all to kill off any hope and desire for change.

"Come on," Pete said, "we'll be late for chow."

After eating four pounds of strawberries, I didn't care whether I was late or not. When I stood up, my head spun around, and my knees were like stilts.

A DOLL NAMED AUGUST

August wasn't writing as often as she used to.

When I thought of her it was kind of rough to remember how green her eyes were. I had a picture of her, but it wasn't in technicolor.

The letters were flattening out too, no more poetry. She really came through on one, though.

". . . I guess you can understand how I feel tonight . . . if only I could fly across the miles of blue water and could just hold you and soothe you, believe me, that's all I'd ever ask of life . . . would be to comfort you . . . this must be a trying time in your life . . . but if only I had things to do over . . . believe me, with all my heart I mean it . . . I would have been more considerate and realized a few things that never entered my head and that I never thought of before or rather that I didn't want to think of them—maybe when this war is over I'll have a chance to prove to you I've changed, do you think I will? . . . and maybe with all this going on you'll understand things about life and, yes, even about me that you didn't know or think about before . . . I know better about things now than I did before . . . I know that this will make the best of you that is possible . . . you will be a better man for all of this, believe me . . . I want you to have faith in me and to know that I'm back of you every inch of the way, pushing you ahead and watching and praying for you always. . . . I just can't go on, you understand, don't you? I'll write you every day. . . ."

But she didn't, and it was a good thing. She was trying to hold on to something that had never been there. She was talking herself into something she didn't really want. She was going through a blank stretch of her life and she had to fill it up with something.

I wasn't worried about her. She'd slip into a new situation and everything would clear up.

She might turn out to be a really good gal for some guy, or she might wind up being a sad sack all the way. She had plenty of both inside her.

She was all gone now. I could remember her clearly enough, but I couldn't bring back the way I felt once when she walked across a room.

If it had mattered, it might have been sad. Funny dame . . . gone now . . . gone for good.

I could still remember Rosemary and Nancy and Kay, and they were still deep in my mind and my blood stream.

But I didn't think of them very often. Five more years would probably put them where August was.

So I didn't have anything at all, that way, just some knocked-out memories, and a twisted dream of the girl from the other side of the mountains, the princess out of the dark.

17

THE SHADOW

We flew four missions in five days. I got fifteen hours of sleep in those five days.

We went to Munich, then way up in the Baltic to a place called Peenemünde, then back to Augsburg.

We were after an airfield at Augsburg.

We took off at 0520 and climbed up through the clouds. It was a broken sky, and there were thin layers of ground fog.

I sang to myself all the way up to oxygen. I did everything without Green telling me. In three missions we already had it down pat.

After the auto-pilot warmed up, Green got it set up. The clouds looked gray and diseased.

By 0548 there was yellow down on top of the soft gray fur, changing slowly to gold and soft orange, with thin streaks of pink above, and one bright arrow of a cloud pointing at the sun.

The ship wasn't climbing worth a damn, and number four was overheating 20 or 30 degrees.

The lead ship got lost and we didn't get formed until almost time to leave the base. The sun came up a brilliant red-orange ball of fire surrounded by thin vapory clouds, and slowly changed to silver, and the clouds became a white snowland set against a mottled sea of England.

We were back on the tail end of the formation. I flew for a while, and when Green took over again the clouds were a puffed layer covered with mist, like Mr. Jordan's country.

At 0742 we were crossing the Belgian coast, over the tide islands. There was a town with a straight-in waterway, and there were dikes.

The crew wasn't making much noise.

The clouds changed into thin curly things. I had to unhook everything and climb down and use the relief tube. What a job that was, and half the time it freezes up and spills all over the catwalk. The cans are better some ways only someone was always kicking them over. The only real solution is cut out all water for two days before a mission.

0815 . . . flak off the right wing.

0825 . . . everything was clear below, with a few chopped up bits of green woods far below. The little towns were surrounded by the thin strips of the farms, all bent out of shape.

0840 . . . another group flew through us. Some wing leader had his head up. There were Forts everywhere, staggering around in prop wash.

0858 . . . we crossed the Rhine.

There was an airfield with planes on it down below.

The cumulus began to grow up over the mountains. We flew down almost to Switzerland before we turned and came back on the airfield.

We were right over the mountains, big valleys, lakes,

snow. I looked for skiers, but maybe the snow was too soft. I looked for fish jumping, but maybe they were in the sack. We were pretty early.

"VHF," Green said.

I listened in.

"Bandits in the target area . . . did you get that, Swordfish Red? . . . bandits in the target area. . . ."

Swordfish Red acknowledged.

"Coming around," I called. It looked like a Focke-Wulf, then I saw another one lower down. "Three o'clock level, coming back," I said.

Back at five he swung in.

"Watch it," I yelled.

Mock opened up on them. The top turret shot one burst.

"They went under," Mock called up.

There was a sky full of flak out at two o'clock, around another combat wing. We were turning.

I looked back and saw a tail and some chunks trickling down.

"Two Forts," Mock said. "One goddamn plane just cut that other one in half."

Two Forts out of our group. Mid-air collision.

We were on the bomb run.

"Doors coming open," Simmers said.

"Doors open," checked from the radio room.

They were shooting white flak, heavy stuff, big red flashes like fighters blowing up.

In the wing ahead of us a Fort powdered. A chunk of it slipped down on to the wing of another. The Tokyo tanks blew. Half a Fort plunged down into the element below. They all went down in a sickening blown-up red mass. Chunks of Forts and tears of flame slowly fell out of the sky.

Then we were out of it, going home.

1114 . . . I finished off my candy bar and took another trip to the relief tube.

1220 . . . we were over the Channel, letting down. There was oil all over the water, maybe bodies floating around. The clouds were thin wisps, blown around, Arctic-looking, cool, and fragile.

1250 . . . we crossed over a bay full of English gunboats, destroyers probably, twenty or more of them.

A Catalina flew across under the formation scarcely moving.

I'd taken along three tortilla-shaped pieces of powdered egg omelet.

"Want some?" I held one out to Green.

He shook his head.

Catalina

I gave Bradley a chance.

He made a gagging noise.

"You don't know what you're missing." They were all right, I was hungry enough.

Green made a nice landing.

Leipzig

The crews scheduled for that haul were waked up around 0300 hours. There was plenty of bitching about that.

I was so tired I felt drunk.

They told us there'd be eggs for breakfast, but there was just bacon without eggs. There was plenty of bitching about that too.

In the equipment hut I heard somebody say, "Today I'm catching up on my sack time."

Some other gunner said, "I slept most of the way to Augsburg yesterday."

Nobody said anything about the Luftwaffe. Leipzig is in there deep, but plenty of gunners bitched about taking extra ammunition. Plenty of gunners didn't take any.

Beach was flying his last mission with Langford's crew.

"We're the last of Lieutenant Newton's gang," he said wanly.

"And I'll be the very last," I said. "Take it easy today."

We had an easy ride in. I didn't feel sleepy. I just felt dazed.

There was soft fuzz over a thin solid overcast going in, but inside Germany the clouds broke up. There was haze under the cumulus and the ground showed pale green through the holes.

"We're way back," Green said.

The group was tucked in nicely, the low squadron was up close, and Langford was doing a pretty job of flying high.

The lead and high groups of our wing looked nice too. But our group, the low, was way back and below. Our wing was the tail end, with most of the 8th up ahead.

The wing had S-ed out and called our group leader to catch up. He didn't.

If I didn't listen to the engine roar it was quiet up there. The sky was a soft sterile blue. Somehow we didn't belong there.

There was death all over that sky, the quiet threat of death, the anesthesia of cold sunlight filled the cockpit.

The lady named Death is a whore. . . . Luck is a lady . . . and so is Death. . . . I don't know why. And there's no telling who they'll go for. Sometimes it's a quiet, gentle, intelligent guy. The Lady Luck strings along with him for a while, and then she hands him over to the lady named Death. Sometimes a guy comes along who can laugh in their faces. The hell with luck, and the hell with death. . . . And maybe they go for it . . . and maybe they don't.

There's no way to tell. If you could become part of the sky you might know . . . because they're always out there. The lady of luck has a lovely face you can never quite see, and her eyes are the night itself, and her hair is probably dark and very lovely . . . but she doesn't give a damn.

And the lady named Death is sometimes lovely too, and sometimes she's a screaming horrible bitch . . . and sometimes she's a quiet one, with soft hands that rest gently on top of yours on the throttles.

The wing leader called up, "We're starting our climb now." We only had a half hour or so until target time.

He hadn't listened. The lead and high groups were already far above us. We were back there alone.

We never caught up after that.

"I don't like this," Green said.

"Tuck it in," somebody said over VHF. "Bandits in the target area."

I was tense and drawn taut. The sky was cold and beautifully aloof.

Green was on interphone and I was on VHF, listening for anything from the lead ship.

I heard a gun open up.

Testing, I decided.

I saw some black puffs and a couple of bright bursts.

Jesus, we're in the flak already, I thought.

Then the guns opened up. Every gun on the ship opened up. A black Focke-Wulf slid under our wing, and rolled over low.

I flipped over on interphone and fear was hot in my throat and cold in my stomach.

"Here they come." It was Mock, I think, cool and easy, like in a church. Then his guns fired steadily.

The air was nothing but black polka dots and firecrackers from the 20-millimeters.

"Keep your eye on 'em. Keep 'em out there. . . ." It was Mock and Bossert.

"Got the one at seven . . ." Bossert or Mock. Steady.

They came through again, coming through from the tail.

I saw two Forts blow up out at four o'clock. Some other group.

A trio of gray ones whipped past under the wing and

rolled away at two o'clock. Black crosses on gray wings
. . . 109's.

A night-fighter Focke-Wulf moved up almost in formation with us, right outside the window, throwing shells
into somebody up ahead. Somebody powdered him.

One came around at ten o'clock . . . and the nose
guns opened up on him. He rolled over and fell away . . .
maybe there was smoke. . . .

The instruments were fine. Green looked okay. My
breath was in short gasps.

"Better give me everything," Green said. Steady voice.

I jacked-up the RPM up to the hilt.

They were queuing up again back at four and six and
eight. A hundred of them . . . maybe two hundred . . .
getting set to come through again . . . fifteen or twenty
abreast. . . .

. . . I looked up at the other wing-ship. The whole
stabilizer was gone. I could see blue sky through there . . .
but the rudder still worked . . . still flapped . . . then his
wing flared up . . . he fell off to the right.

We were flying off Langford, but he was gone . . .
sagging off low at three o'clock. Green slid us in under the
lead squadron. Langford was in a dive . . . four or five
planes were after him . . . coming in . . . letting them
have it . . . swinging out . . . and coming in again . . .
Beach was in that ball . . . poor goddamn Beach. . . .

"Here they come!"

"Four o'clock level."

"Take that one at six."

All the guns were going again.

There wasn't any hope at all . . . just waiting for it
. . . just sitting there hunched up . . . jerking around to
check the right side . . . jerking back to check the instruments . . . everything okay . . . just waiting for it. . . .

They came through six times, I guess . . . maybe five
. . . maybe seven . . . queuing up back there . . . coming
in . . . throwing those 20's in there.

. . . we were hit . . .

. . . the whole low squadron was gone . . . blown up
. . . burned up . . . shot to hell . . . one guy got out of
that.

. . . we were the only ones left in the high . . .
tucked in under the lead. The lead squadron was okay . . .
we snuggled up almost under the tail guns. They were
firing steadily . . . the shell cases were dropping down and
going through the cowling . . . smashing against the plexiglass . . . chipping away at the windshields . . . coming
steady . . . coming all the time . . . then his guns must
have burned out . . .

. . . there were a few 51's back there . . . four against
a hundred . . . maybe eight. . . .

"Don't shoot that 51," Mock again, cool as hell . . .

I punched the wheel forward. A burning plane was
nosing over us.

Green nodded, kept on flying. . . .

The guns were going . . . not all of them any more
. . . some of them were out . . . burned out . . . maybe.

And then it was over. They went away.

We closed up and dropped our bombs.

Six out of twelve gone.

We turned off the target, waiting for them . . . knowing they'd be back . . . cold . . . waiting for them. . . .

There was a flow to it . . . we were moving . . . we
were always moving . . . sliding along through the dead
sky. . . .

I flicked back to VHF.

No bandits called off.

Then, I heard, ". . . is my wing on fire? . . . will you check to see if my wing is on fire? . . ."

He gave his call sign. It was the lead ship.

We were right underneath. We pulled up even closer.

"You're okay," I broke the safety wire on the transmitter. "You're okay . . . baby . . . your wing is okay. No smoke . . . no flame . . . stay in there, baby."

It was more of a prayer.

". . . I'm bailing out my crew. . . ."

I couldn't see any flame. I wasn't sure it was the same plane. But they were pulling out to the side.

All my buddies. Maurie . . . Uggie . . .

I told Green. "We better get back to the main group . . . we better get back there fast . . ."

We banked over. I saw the rear door come off and flip away end over end in the slipstream. Then the front door, then something else . . . maybe a guy doing a delayed jump. It didn't look like a guy very much.

It must have been set up on automatic pilot. It flew along out there for half an hour. If they jumped they were delayed jumps.

Maybe they made it.

We found a place under the wing lead.

I reached over and touched Green. What a guy. Then I felt the control column. Good airplane . . . still flying . . . still living. . . .

Everybody was talking.

Nobody knew what anybody said.

There was a sort of beautiful dazed wonder in the air . . .

. . . still here. . . . Still living . . . still breathing.

And then it came through . . . the thought of all those guys . . . those good guys . . . cooked and smashed and down there somewhere, dead or chopped up or headed for some Stalag.

We were never in that formation. We were all alone, trailing low.

From the day you first get in a 17 they say formation flying is the secret.

They tell you over and over. Keep those planes tucked in and you'll come home.

The ride home was easy. They never came back.

The sky was a soft unbelievable blue. The land was green, never so green.

When we got away from the Continent we began to come apart. Green took off his mask.

There weren't any words, but we tried to say them.

"Jesus, you're here," I said.

"I'm awfully proud of them," he said quietly.

Bradley came down out of the turret. His face was nothing but teeth. I mussed up his hair, and he beat on me.

The interphone was jammed.

". . . all I could do was pray . . . and keep praying." McAvoy had to stay in the radio room the whole time, seeing nothing, doing nothing. . . .

"You can be the chaplain," Mock said. His voice was just the same, only he was laughing a little now.

". . . if they say go tomorrow . . . I'll hand in my wings. . . . I'll hand in every other goddamn thing . . . but I won't fly tomorrow . . ." Tolbert was positive.

. . . if Langford went down . . . that meant Fletch . . . Fletch and Johnny O'Leary and Beach . . .

. . . and all the others. . . . Maurie had long black eyelashes, and sort of Persian's eyes . . . sort of the walking symbol of sex . . . and what a guy . . . maybe he made it . . . maybe he got out. . . .

201

It was low tide. The clouds were under us again, almost solid, and then I saw a beach through a hole . . . white sand and England.

There was never anywhere as beautiful as that.

We were home.

Green made a sweet landing. We opened up the side windows and looked around. Everything looked different. There was too much light, too much green . . . just too much . . .

We were home. . . .

They sent us out to get knocked off and we came home.

And then we taxied past E-East.

"Jesus, that's Langford," I grabbed Green.

It was. Even from there we could see they were shot to hell. Their tail was all shot up . . . one wing was ripped and chopped away.

Green swung around into place, and I cut the engines.

. . . we were home . . .

There were empty spaces where ships were supposed to be, where they'd be again in a day, as soon as ATC could fly them down.

We started to talk to people. There were all kinds of people. Jerry, a crew chief, came up and asked us about the guys on the other wing. We told him. Blown up.

. . . honest to God . . . we were really home. . . .

The 20-millimeter hit our wing . . . blew up inside . . . blew away part of the top of number two gas tank . . . blew hell out of everything inside there . . . puffed out the leading edge . . . blew out an inspection panel.

We didn't even lose any gas.

We didn't even blow up.

I stood back by the tail and looked at the hole. I could

feel the ground, and I wanted to take my shoes off. Every time I breathed, I knew it.

I could look into the sky over the hangar and say thank you to the lady of the luck. She stayed.

I was all ripped apart. Part of me was dead, and part of me was wild, ready to take off, and part of me was just shaky and twisted and useless.

Maybe I told it a thousand times.

I could listen to myself. I could talk, and start my voice going, and step back and listen to it.

I went down to Thompson's room, and he listened. He listened a couple of times.

It was a pretty quiet place. Eight ships out of a group is a quiet day at any base.

Colonel Terry just got married. Thompson didn't know about it. I went back to my room and sat across the room from Langford and kept telling myself it was him.

"When I saw you there were at least eight of them," I said. "Just coming in, and pulling out, and coming in." I showed him with my hands.

Then Fletch came in.

Then I thought about Beach.

Beach got three at least. He shot up every shell he had, and got three.

He came over after interrogation.

"I guess they can't kill us Denver guys," he said. He didn't believe it either. He was all through.

"Jesus," I said, "I sure thought they had you."

Green came in with O'Leary.

"I knew you were down," O'Leary said. "I told everyone."

Green smiled. He looked okay. "We're on pass," he said quietly. "Let's get out of here."

I wanted to touch him again. I wanted to tell him I was glad I was on his crew, and it was the best goddamn crew I'd ever heard of, but I didn't say anything, and he didn't either.

I got out my typewriter and started a letter to my folks.

And then it came in again . . . all those guys . . . all those good guys . . . shot to hell . . . or captured . . . or hiding there waiting for it.

. . . waiting for it. . . .

Then I came apart, and cried like a little kid . . . I could watch myself, and hear myself, and I couldn't do a goddamn thing.

. . . just pieces of a guy . . . pieces of bertstiles all over the room . . . maybe some of the pieces were still over there.

And then it was all right. I went in and washed my face. Green was calling up about trains, standing there in his shorts.

"I think the boys need a rest," he said. "You going in?"

"I'll meet you in London at high noon," I said. "Lobby of the Regent Palace."

"Okay," he said. "Get a good night's sleep."

"Meet you there," I said.

But I didn't.

They sent me to the Flak House. There was an opening, and the squadron sent me.

18

SO TO FINISH UP

It is summer and there is war all over the world . . . the war has spread from Normandy to Brittany and the American columns are swinging in toward Paris. There is still plenty of war in Russia. The same war is still going on in the islands and in the sky over Japan.

I can only think about it in terms of moments and chunks and stretches of eternity measured in minutes . . .

So far I've lived through it. So far the lady of luck has let me come through.

There is hope as bright as the sun that it will end soon. I hope it does. I hope the hell it does.

It will be a long time before I have made up my mind about this war.

I am an American. I was lucky enough to be born below the mountains in Colorado. But some day I would like to be able to say I live in the world and let it go at that.

The trouble with me is, I don't know even how to

start to build my share of the one world. So if I get through this, I will have to get on the ball and learn something about economics and people and things.

If that is vague, it is because I do not know where to start to be specific. In the end it is only people that count, all the people in the whole world. Any land is beautiful to someone. Any land is worth fighting for to someone. So it isn't the land.

It is the people.

That is what the war is about, I think. Beyond that I can't go very far. So if we can get through this war I'll get started. . . .

ABOUT THE AUTHOR

BERT STILES was a student at Colorado College in 1942 when he joined the American Army Air Force. He received his commission in November 1943, and went overseas to Great Britain in March 1944. He was awarded the Air Medal and the Distinguished Flying Cross and was a veteran of thirty-five bomber missions. Instead of returning to America when leave was due to him, he requested to be transferred to fighters. On November 26, 1944, he was shot down in a P-51 on an escort mission to Hanover. He died at the age of 23.

THE REMARKABLE #1 BESTSELLER
NOW IN PAPERBACK

JOHN LE CARRÉ

THE LITTLE DRUMMER GIRL

Here is the terrifying adventure of Charlie, a young actress forced to play the ultimate role in the secret pursuit of a dangerous and elusive terrorist leader. This is John le Carré's richest and most thrilling novel yet, plunging us into entirely new labyrinths of intrigue, into the dark heart of modern-day terrorism.

"A TRIUMPH." —*Time*

"AN IRRESISTIBLE BOOK . . . CHARLIE IS THE ULTI-MATE DOUBLE AGENT." —*The New York Times*

Buy THE LITTLE DRUMMER GIRL, on sale April 1, 1984, wherever Bantam paperbacks are sold, or use the handy coupon below for ordering:

"A ONE-OF-A-KIND NOVEL OF SUSPENSE LIKE *THE DAY OF THE JACKAL*"
—Steve Shagan, author of THE CIRCLE

BALEFIRE
by Kenneth Goddard

Brutal, inexplicable killings suddenly terrorize a city on the California coast. Stunned and confused, the police feel powerless to defend their city, their families and themselves against these meticulously planned "random" attacks by an unseen predator. Until they realize that the havoc might be a cover-up to something even more shocking. As tensions edge toward panic, a select team of investigators and crime lab specialists steps outside the law to fight back. But soon, these dedicated men and woman fall prey to the elusive Thanatos, a superbly capable professional killer, a relentless human hunter whose greatest weapon may also be his fatal flaw— fear itself.

Read BALEFIRE, on sale April 15, 1984, wherever Bantam paperbacks are sold or use the handy coupon below for ordering:

Join the Allies on the Road to Victory
BANTAM WAR BOOKS

THE AVIATOR'S BOOKSHELF
THE CLASSICS OF FLYING

The books that aviators, test pilots, and astronauts feel tell the most about the skills that launched mankind on the adventure of flight. These books bridge man's amazing progress, from the Wright brothers to the first moonwalk.

- [ ] **THE WRIGHT BROTHERS by Fred C. Kelly** (23962-7 • $2.95)
  Their inventive genius was enhanced by their ability to learn how to fly their machines.
- [ ] **THE FLYING NORTH by Jean Potter** (23946-5 • $2.95)
  The Alaskan bush pilots flew in impossible weather, frequently landing on sandbars or improvised landing strips, flying the early planes in largely uninhabited and unexplored land.
- [ ] **THE SKY BEYOND by Sir Gordon Taylor** (23949-X • $2.95)
  Transcontinental flight required new machines piloted by skilled navigators who could pinpoint tiny islands in the vast Pacific—before there were radio beacons and directional flying aids.
- [ ] **THE WORLD ALOFT by Guy Murchie** (23947-3 • $2.95)
  The book recognized as *The Sea Round Us* for the vaster domain—the Air. Mr. Murchie, a flyer, draws from history, mythology and many sciences. The sky is an ocean, filled with currents and wildlife of its own. A tribute to, and a celebration of, the flyers' environment.
- [ ] **CARRYING THE FIRE by Michael Collins** (23948-1 • $3.50)
  "The best written book yet by any of the astronauts."—*Time Magazine*. Collins, the Gemini 10 and Apollo 11 astronaut, gives us a picture of the joys of flight and the close-in details of the first manned moon landing.
- [ ] **THE LONELY SKY by William Bridgeman with Jacqueline Hazard** (23950-3 • $3.50)
  The test pilot who flew the fastest and the highest. The excitement of going where no one has ever flown before by a pilot whose careful study and preparation was matched by his courage.

Read all of the books in THE AVIATOR'S BOOKSHELF

Prices and availability subject to change without notice

Buy them at your bookstore or use this handy coupon for ordering:

Bantam Books, Inc., Dept. WW4, 414 East Golf Road, Des Plaines, Ill. 60016

Please send me the books I have checked above. I am enclosing $_____ (please add $1.25 to cover postage and handling). Send check or money order —no cash or C.O.D.'s please.

Mr/Mrs/Miss _____

Address_____

City_____ State/Zip_____

WW4—5/84

Please allow four to six weeks for delivery. This offer expires 11/84.

SPECIAL
MONEY SAVING
OFFER

Now you can have an up-to-date listing of Bantam's hundreds of titles plus take advantage of our unique and exciting bonus book offer. A special offer which gives you the opportunity to purchase a Bantam book for only 50¢. Here's how!

By ordering any five books at the regular price per order, you can also choose any other single book listed (up to a $4.95 value) for just 50¢. Some restrictions do apply, but for further details why not send for Bantam's listing of titles today!

Just send us your name and address plus 50¢ to defray the postage and handling costs.

BANTAM BOOKS, INC.
Dept. FC, 414 East Golf Road, Des Plaines, Ill 60016

Mr./Mrs./Miss/Ms. _____
(please print)

Address _____

City_____ State_____ Zip_____

FC—3/84